Y.M. Brignoni

Dragonfly Women

©04052022

Soledad was boiling lentil stew for dinner when she felt a sudden desire to go down the hill to pick wild berries. Even from the heights of her home, she had fallen victim to the seduction of the scented fruit of the valley. Forgetting she was cooking, she opened the door and walked out as if hypnotized. She descended the long stairs made of flat and irregular stones, until she reached the plain. She walked away with her basket, unaware of the extensive distance she created between her house and her berry picking. Despite suffering the lash of the violent sun on her back, she surrendered to the tasteful magic offered by the sweet ruby colored fruit.

A second of awareness shook her with a piercing chill, reminding her of the boiling stew. She turned around and looked back. Soledad could barely see her home. Not only did she start fearing the distance she had walked, but also the imprecise time it had taken her to get there. She couldn't understand how she could have been so distracted, particularly in her condition. She took a deep breath and turned back to get home as quickly as possible. After only three steps, she was surprised by a brutal abdominal contraction. As her belly shifted in a violent earthquake-like motion, her knees faltered sending her body to the rich ground of the valley.

Soledad breathed deeply, attempting to control her cramps, as she crawled to a rock that lay at the foot of a leafy tree providing generous shade. She slid her body over the rock like a wounded reptile and managed to sit on the grass of the plain. Then, pain brutally squeezed her insides as she felt the dampness of the amniotic fluid running down her left leg. She clenched her teeth and then, crying out, she ripped her under garments off. She saw her blood spew like the fiery magma of an erupting volcano. Soledad was no longer thinking of the porridge on the stove. The shock of unexpected labor had scrambled her list of priorities; she had miscalculated her due date.

Her belly kept on constricting like the walls of her wooden shack in winter; every single crackle, a cry of pain. She felt naturally drugged, as if viewing everything through an unreal and transparent veil. An hour had gone by before a voracious squeeze propelled the baby onto a comfortable bedspread of fresh grass. Yet, Soledad was still in pain, and she waited, sweating and breathing as she continued her process. Then, she pushed again and another baby crowned. She had to move away to avoid hitting her first born with the oncoming one. She could only smile at the unexpected event of having twins, for she had never been examined by a doctor. At that very moment when she started to feel somewhat blissful, she looked toward the mountain where she lived. She saw a long funnel of black smoke expanding in the distance. Then, her smile turned to sadness and desperation.

"Good God, my house is burning. What do I do now?" she thought, closing her eyes in disbelief.

She knelt without difficulty, allowing the skirt of her dress to flow down her thighs. She then looked at her twins covered in blood and a heavy coating that she believed was sort of cheesy paste. The dragonflies of the field had perched on the newborns as if they were tiny birds. However, Soledad noticed that they did not stand on their heads, faces, or hands; only on their torsos and legs. The tormented mother searched for a piece of cloth or paper to clean her daughters. When she realized there was nothing available around her, she decided to swing her arms to scare away the dragonflies. Then, she lifted both her daughters and pressed them against her chest. She carried them to the stream and placed them on the riverbank, where she washed them with fresh water until their skin glistened. Nonetheless, the winged creatures followed their course, compelled by some unknown natural instinct.

The mother protected the naked little girls against the flight by holding them tight to her bosom, right under her dress to keep them warm while she walked in the direction of her village. As she approached the remains of her shack, there were only ashes and embers left, which gradually died down after the inferno had devoured her humble abode. Soledad moaned and trembled, not knowing where to go, or how to protect her little ones. In her desperate mental state, she fled the familiar area; the swarm of dragonflies still following behind her.

Night was upon her. Weak and disoriented, she had no idea where she was. Afraid, she kept on holding her naked little girls tight to her chest. After walking a long while towards town, she saw a lit residence in an unfamiliar neighborhood. She knocked on the door three times, and waited for a few minutes, until a woman in her fifties finally opened the door. Soledad managed to pull each baby from under the top of her dress, and hand each one to the lady.

"Don't let the dragonflies in" she said before collapsing.

The perplexed woman followed the instructions of the young mother. Upon awakening, Soledad found herself clean and in a very comfortable bed. She couldn't hear anything around her, only an uninterrupted silence. Her skin crawled at the thought that she had lost her mind and that she had left her two newborns on the loose. She did not know their whereabouts, nor how long she had been asleep and senseless in the hands of a stranger. She had just opened her eyes after what seemed to be a long dream. Then, a while after, she saw the woman who gave her shelter, approaching her. Before Soledad could speak, the lady smiled softly at her. Her gentle gesture conveyed great peace and confidence to the new mother.

"You've had a very high fever since yesterday, but we have already treated you," she said, comforting Soledad with the silky touch of her hand.

"What about my daughters?" she asked, very concerned.

"They are doing better than you. They're sleeping in the room next to yours. Do you want me to bring them to you, or do you prefer to go see them?"

"I'm going," Soledad answered, trying to get up.

She was still unsteady on her feet due to dehydration and blood loss during her delivery. Therefore, the lady helped her up without complaint, bearing the pain of the young woman's weight on her damaged bones. Moreover, she served as support for her to walk steady and with confidence. Upon reaching the room, Soledad saw her daughters very well cared for, fed, and clothed.

"I feel so bad!" she said in a trembling voice, feeling deeply humiliated.

"What were you doing, darling? Were you in danger?" asked the lady.

"No, I wasn't. Maybe yes."

"Well, I hope everything goes well for you. My name is Virginia and that's Francisco" she said pointing to her husband the minute she saw him approaching.

Greatly embarrassed, the young mother thanked them. The man smiled at her, lowering his kind eyes for a second. Sixteen-year- old Soledad, who did not have the strength to drag her body to the room where she had awakened, asked the couple to help her back to bed. She was still distraught while she rested; her thoughts hammering her tortured mind. She couldn't return to the town where no one awaited her. Her husband had abandoned her for another woman the minute he learned of her pregnancy. Although he showed up repentant after six months of her waiting, she could not forgive his actions, and had asked him to leave. Both her husband and her little house were full of excessive mystery. Everything was lost in between those four walls: love, health, happiness, kitchen items, sheets, and even pillows. The only thing that remained was the magical beauty of the garden and the lonely girl, turned woman, who cultivated it.

Her garden soothed her with its yellow allamandas, orchids, bougainvillea, poppies, and its fragrant roses of many colors and shades. Thinking of her flowers, Soledad exhaled and closed her eyes.

She surrendered to delirium, carried on the wings of the lethargy of an existential dream. Scenes from her childhood, her adolescence, and her marriage, paraded on the reel of her vivid dreams. They drifted in and out of her memory at the speed of a storm's violet lightning. She remembered her mother's love, her personal strengths and weaknesses, and her father's rigor. Then, she recalled her husband Luis Segarra, once again. He was vivacious and gentle, but uncommitted; therefore, very absent from home.

Soledad, always protected by her parents until she was handed to her husband, saw her life turn opposite to what she had expected. Due to her emotional immaturity and her present precarious circumstances, she did not believe herself capable of raising her two daughters. She had not planned to get pregnant and the surprise of her condition had seemed more of a hallucination than a reality. Realizing that as a mother, she would have unknown and overwhelming responsibilities, she began to cry and sweat profusely. She felt she was suffocating; the air around her too dense to breathe in. A cold, continuous shudder took over her body, paralyzing her face into a frown. She remained motionless for a few minutes. Suddenly, she snapped out of it. She got up and fled like a swift beast chased by a dozen hunters. No one would have been able to prevent her from running away. Without contemplation, and feeling lost, she jumped off a cliff into the wild waters of the river.

Her body was never found. No one ever asked for her, nor did they claim the newborns, even after broadcasts and government published edicts in the country's newspapers. Weeks passed without any information on Soledad, from the girls' father, or any direct family member. Virginia and Francisco turned the fraternal twins over to the authorities. The state had custody until the waiting period expired, before placing them for adoption. Although the couple would have liked to raise them, they both lacked the health to do so. Francisco had suffered two violent heart attacks and Virginia had endured severe arthritis for years. Soledad disappeared without knowing that in order to put her to bed and wash her, after she collapsed at the front door, Virginia had to carry her with the assistance of her neighbors. Then again, Virginia and Francisco never found out that Soledad had attempted to commit suicide. Nor did they know that her first name *loneliness* was an appropriate adjective to describe the circumstances that prompted her decision to abandon her current reality.

✳✳✳

Silvana and Marina were adopted within two months of being placed in the custody of the government. Felipa Isabel Iglesias and Rogelio Guzmán, both a little over forty years old and married for two decades, were delighted by the idea of adopting the Mexican twins. The potential parents had requested adoption procedural assistance from a relative who lived in the girls' country of origin. They submitted all the legal documents through their representative, and attended the required interviews to complete the process. Before finalizing the adoption, the Guzmán-Iglesias received a phone call from a social worker. Among other data, she informed them that the girls attracted dragonflies when exposed to natural areas. When Felipa Isabel asked her for logical reasons, Mrs. Gutiérrez only explained what Virginia had written in her narration about the flying creatures.

"Apparently, these girls kept traces of blood for a long time after being briefly washed in the waters of a stream."

"And what does all that have to do with it?" Felipa asked.

"The mother believed that they were attracted by the fishy smell of the blood residues on babies' skin, because when dragonflies are water nymphs, they eat very small fish."

"Nonsense! Forgive me, Mrs. Gutiérrez, but that is crazy countryside superstition. If they are dragonflies, they are no longer nymphs. That just doesn't make sense."

Mrs. Gutiérrez did not answer, and at that moment decided to end the conversation. Like the potential adopting mother, she didn't believe either any of the anecdotes about the dragonflies. As a government worker, she was supposed to be impartial. She smiled, and informed Felipa that her job was only to notify prospective parents of all available information regarding their adoption. To her that call was another formality, just part of a series of tasks and requirements to be fulfilled before adoption. However, since they were prominent people, she had been informed by the higher-ups that the Guzmán-Iglesias' investigation needed to be a fairly accelerated process.

She was told that they had an impressive standing in their community due to their great wealth. They were the owners of several well-known and widely consumed brands of alcoholic beverages in the United States. As a result of that fact, some higher government official had concluded that they were honest people of exceptional virtue. Therefore, the adoption investigation was completed and approved without any delay. After several large payments and a four-week waiting period, during which the application was processed, the Guzmán-Iglesias would welcome the five-month-old twins into their home.

Their representative delivered them in the evening after the day of their final adoption approval. Then, he was set off to a wonderful luxury vacation, courtesy of the new parents. The entering of the little ones at the residence in Miami resulted in a great celebration, just a couple of hours after their arrival in the city. A month prior to their homecoming, the couple had hired an event coordinating agency to plan a reception party for more than a hundred guests. Both, the entire Guzmán and the Iglesias families had been invited to attend. Nobody missed the celebration. The governor, the mayor and other government dignitaries, also showed up. Even the bishop was present at the activity, just to bless the parents and their infants. Renowned artists came to sing and participate. Neighbors, friends and those who claimed to know the family, made an appearance. All the guests were served delicacies of every kind and the best drinks from their family business.

There was music all night and even a closing show at two in the morning; a regal act with multiple fireworks from China. Miami's largest social celebration of 1961 was immortalized on the covers of the city's most popular magazines and all its well-known newspapers. The activity was one of the most photographed social events that year, and for sure, the most talked about in the city for two consecutive seasons. However, the reality after the party was that the arrival of the twins changed the world of the Guzmán-Iglesias. Having gone to bed at three o'clock in the morning, the couple ignored the particular schedule of the newborns.

The nanny they hired weeks before, showed up four hours later. She knocked on the door countless times, but the new parents had slipped into a deep slumber after the eventful night and copious drinking. Meanwhile, deafening screams caused by hunger and the need for care were heard from the girls' room. The nanny could hear them outside, but the Guzmán-Iglesias only heard them as part of a morning nightmare that both shared in their deep dreaming stage. After an hour of the nanny's shouting, the butler got up, ready to begin his work. He entered the main house from his little house in the immense courtyard of the great residence, and heard the persistent bells coming from the front door of the mansion. He looked with his right eye through the peephole and saw a rather young woman with a sullen face. He immediately opened and greeted her. The nanny offered him a forced smile, trying to swallow the feast of anger she had endured for an hour.

"Hello. I'm Serena Matos, the nanny. I got here shortly before seven and have been ringing that doorbell for *an eternity*. I've been hearing the babies crying all morning and nobody has done anything! Can you explain to me what is happening?"

"Excuse me, Miss Matos. My name is Manuel and I am the butler of the house. All I can do is to ask you to please go upstairs and tend to the girls. If you don't want to come back after today, please talk to Miss Felipa."

The nanny said nothing and proceeded to the nursery. She found them as red as ripe tomatoes; so much had they been crying. Their diapers were more than saturated with feces and urine, not having been changed for long hours. Serena tried to appease her indignation at the conditions in which she found the girls, so they wouldn't feel the negative energy of her discontent. She took several deep breaths and managed to calm herself. She cleaned and bathed the babies immediately and took them down to the first floor to feed them. After locating the kitchen, she opened the stocked refrigerator, but there were no baby groceries. Therefore, she boiled two eggs as the first food. Then she made baby food with fresh fruit, mixed with warm cow's milk and purified water. Unable to find carriers or high chairs to accommodate and feed the girls, she had to improvise again. She placed them on the sofa, in a slightly reclining but well protected position.

"What kind of savages are these people?" she wondered silently, trying to honor her name, which meant *serene*. For the most part, her name represented her personality, except for the times when outrage was justified.

Manuel, the butler, looked at her from a distance, feeling embarrassed by the lack of responsibility of his employers. He observed the skill of the young woman and the loving care given to the twins. She even fed them simultaneously. She gave a teaspoon of well mashed egg to one and another teaspoon to the second, thus maintaining a rhythmic system. She would smile at them whenever they ate voraciously, and looked into their eyes as they received the food. They seemed to appreciate her care with clearly manifested facial expressions. She also noticed that whenever she spoke sweetly to them, they smiled in happy response. Then, sensing so much beauty and sensitivity in their gratitude, Serena was captivated with the gift of twin love that she received.

Two hours later, Elena, the cook, briefly met her. She apologized to Serena for having to greet her in a hurry. Just like Manuel, she had worked all night during the party. Exhausted as she was, she had limited time to prepare breakfast for the Guzmán-Iglesias. She was well aware of her bosses' habit of getting up late after celebrations. She also knew the exact moment they would come down to the breakfast table. As expected, few minutes later, Felipa Isabel and Rogelio showed up. By then, the nanny had already been inside the mansion for three hours.

Upon seeing Serena from a distance, Felipa Isabel remembered that she had hired her two weeks before the welcoming party. The thought triggered the fact that shortly before the celebration, she and her husband had welcomed her two adopted daughters.

"My God! Rogelio! That's the babysitter!"

"A babysitter?" he said totally oblivious.

"The one we hired for our twins!" Felipa Isabel said still in awe.

"True! How could we forget? It was because of them that we celebrated the party," Rogelio recalled.

Serena couldn't believe what she was hearing. She was trying to control her temper, when Manuel looked at her as though asking her to forgive their emotional insufficiency. She responded by lowering her eyes as she nodded in understanding. Then she walked towards them.

"Hello. I'm sure you remember me. I am Serena, the babysitter. I would like to inform you that I found no strollers, no high chairs, no clothes, no diapers… not much of anything for the girls. They've been bare-ass for hours."

"That's a shame, Serena! Look, I was going to buy all that, but I admit that with all the party requirements, we forgot everything else," Felipa answered while displaying a rehearsed sorrowful gesture.

"So then, what do you propose I do, Mrs. Guzmán-Iglesias?" Serena replied slightly sarcastically, keeping in mind Manuel's silent petition.

Felipa solved the situation by waving her hand to Manuel, asking to join them. Then, she told Serena to write a list of all the items she needed for the girls and to hand it to the butler immediately. Serena, who was already ahead of Felipa, gave her a list she had written earlier, while assessing the lack of supplies. Felipa looked at her from head to toe, and then handed the list to Manuel. He left to call Felipa's favorite department store to place her order.

The employees at the store already knew to select the best of any product for her right away, for her driver to pick within a half hour. On this occasion, Manuel asked them to have the order expedited because Felipa had an impending spa appointment for a massage and hairstyling. Therefore, it had to be done right away.

"Serena dear, you will soon have everything you need. Problem solved!" Felipa shrugged while looking at Serena in the eye, stone-faced, after having watched Manuel placing the order.

"And you, darling, you need to share the experience. Remember that you're a father now. Go kiss the girls, and then onto your golf tournament" Felipa said to Rogelio, smiling while raising her eyebrows.

"Hmmm" he uttered while reading his newspaper.

"They are asleep now. Would you like to see them, ma'am?" Serena asked her.

"Not now. Maybe later in the afternoon. I need more coffee and a hot bath to feel better. You're going to live here, aren't you, Serena?"

"Well, ma'am…They were not very clear about that in the agency, but they anticipated that it might be so."

"Well, I'm glad, and if you didn't bring your things, Carlos will take you to get them later."

"Carlos?"

"He's the driver."

"Sir, do you want to go kiss your daughters?" Serena asked Rogelio.

"No, you already heard Felipa Isabel. I'm going to play golf."

"Miss Felipa, what are the girls' names?

"I have the papers with the photos, Serena. Before I leave, I'll give them to you. Look, nobody asked me last night. I would have remembered otherwise. Ok?" she said waving her hand dismissively.

After that first conversation, the nanny understood that she had arrived into a very deficient home, where parents lacked maturity despite their obvious age. She recognized that all responsibilities would fall on her and that the road ahead would be more arduous than in any of her previous experiences. Aware of the difficult days ahead, she went up to the twins' room and opened the windows to let in the sweet breezes of May. Serena admired the beauty of the lands surrounded by abundant trees, which offered privacy to the impressive Guzmán-Iglesias' mansion. The sheer curtains undulating in the girls' comfortable room were lifted by the cool flower-scented wind. Serena closed her eyes, as she reveled in the warm kiss of spring on her fresh rosy cheeks. In the meantime, she did not notice that a troop of many rainbow-colored dragonflies propelled by the breeze, had entered the room. A collective flutter produced by their iridescent silken wings, alerted her to the invasion. She saw them land on the babies, who laughed joyfully feeling the tickling of their legs.

Serena was scared at first, but she remembered having read about dragonflies in the babies' adoption file given to her by the new parents when she was hired. She recalled the reference to birth blood in relation to the flying insects, which seemed pure fantasy to her. She, who had a keener sense of smell than all the people she knew, felt like finding out the truth. Then she hesitated and decided not to proceed.

"It's all nonsense. It's not feasible…not possible," she thought, feeling indecisive.

However, always a very pragmatic person, she made the final decision to put her sense of smell to the test once again. She approached the babies and with both hands, scared all the dragonflies away. Then, she closed the windows. She looked at the girls and they looked very happy, making beautiful little sounds. Then, she grabbed Silvana, the larger of the two, and breathed deeply onto her skin to determine if there was actually any scent. That intense inhalation seemed to draw a faint river fish smell from the depths of her pores. Serena put the baby back in her crib and grabbed Marina to confirm if she also carried the odor. She could identify the same odor again, lingering beneath the surface of the skin. Serena was in awe. She couldn't believe that the dragonflies could sense their primordial nymph stage from the babies' dermis.

"Incredible! It's like they're coming home!" Serena thought.

Despite her disbelief, she knew that nature itself has an ethereal synchronization and a perfect balance, often not understood. The dragonflies were only responding to their innate instinct of recognizing a familiar chemistry. Serena decided that under no circumstances she would discuss her experience with anyone. From that moment on, she would take every conceivable measure in her power to prevent other people, including the parents, from discovering the babies' attraction of dragonflies. She also decided to keep them fully dressed, with long-sleeved shirts and long-legged pants, stockings, and closed shoes; except on special dragonfly meeting days.

✳✳✳

The twins grew up witnessing daily fights and agitated discussions between Rogelio and Felipa Isabel. Through their first three years of life, they had seen the same aggressive couple dynamic in some tv soap operas that Elena used to watch while cooking. They assumed that Felipa Isabel and Rogelio were a part of those stories; tv series they could see without the need for a black and white television. They just watched with curiosity as the new and repeated scenes of the live show played out at home. The mansion's actors always carried in their right hands a wide-mouthed glass, half-filled with a coppery substance that seemed to be neither milk nor juice.

On a particular day, the girls noticed inside of a large room's furniture, those particular cups they had seen so many times. They looked into each other's eyes for about twenty seconds; enough time for the two of them to plot a detailed plan for that very night. At three in the morning, when everyone slept soundly, they got up. They crept down the stairs, like two clever little kittens, to reach the living room. They walked hand in hand to the adjacent room where the Guzmán-Iglesias' bar was located. Upon entering, Silvana quickly climbed into the armchair next to the floor lamp, placed closely to the entryway of the room. Wasting no time, Marina climbed onto a small stool to reach the second highest drawer of the bulky bar furniture. She managed to open it wide enough to be able to climb, right foot first. Then the little girl began to ascend as if she were climbing Mount Everest. She was attempting to get to the platform that gave access to the liquor shelf at the top.

Silvana placed herself at a lower level on the same bench, waiting for Marina to detect the right bottle. Despite being firmly planted on the counter, the bottle she wanted was towards the back of the shelf. She had to stand on her tippy toes like a ballet dancer to reach the bottle with her little right arm. Although extremely difficult, she managed to grab it by its neck and drag it forward little by little until she was able to hold it firmly. Then, she leaned over the counter and handed it to Silvana from above. In that transfer, the bottle slipped from one hand to the other and almost fell. Silvana managed to grab it; all the while she could hear her heartbeat racing like a stampede of wild horses. They both took a moment to breathe and compose themselves, knowing that had the bottle fallen, the noise of the glass would have awakened the adults.

After the scary start, it was time to find the glasses to drink the dark golden liquid. Marina squatted to crawl across the counter to the other end. The sink was right in the middle of the path. Then, she saw two empty glasses inside the belly of the large porcelain pot. With just one look, she let Silvana know that it was better to take the ones that were available, instead of going forward to the other side. While Marina took out the whiskey glasses from the sink, Silvana put the bottle on a table next to the bar. Later, Marina handed her the glasses one by one. Silvana got off the bench each time to secure both of them with great care, putting them next to the bottle.

Marina returned to her starting point and descended on her back, tapping with her right foot until she found the edge of the slightly open drawer. Once in a stable position, she went down the stool onto the floor. By the time she got to her sister, Silvana had already served just a little of the liquid in each glass. After having smelled the disgusting scent, she decided that one sip was more than enough to determine if it was worth drinking. After both girls tasted it, they spat it back into their glasses. Never having experienced such a foul taste, they emptied the contents of the glasses onto a plant in the room. Then, they repeated the entire initial climbing procedure to return the bottle and glasses to their place. Once done, they climbed the stairs to their bedroom and lay down as if nothing had happened.

The next day, Serena went to get them ready for a walk in the gardens. She found them dressed in shorts and tank tops, and she smiled at them, aware that they knew where they were going. They enjoyed playing and hiding in the immense courtyard of the mansion; twenty acres of pure green on the outskirts of the metropolis. The property included a pristine water stream that exalted the beauty of the lands with its shallow white bends. It was the perfect place for the little ones to enjoy their free nature and their particular harmony with dragonflies. On this occasion, as on many others, Marina decided to imitate bird songs. Although at times she did so as a manifestation of concern, in nature it was always her expression of joy and communion with the multicolored winged beings.

While that aspect of the girls was somewhat strange for Serena, she was aware of the deep joy and peace they felt. Observing them in nature laughing with the dragonflies was proof enough that, at least once a week, they deserved the replenishing effect of such a unique activity. Therefore, the nanny had included those special days in the calendar, from the first time the dragonflies came in droves through the windows of the children's room. Not only did she make it fun for them, it also became a promise she kept over the years.

After having experienced so many beautiful things with the twins, Serena felt time was slipping away too fast. In only six months the twins would turn five. They had grown up to understand everything around them more clearly. Thus, they witnessed many changes in the mansion. Manuel, who was only allowed to be loving and gentle to them from the distance, one day resigned out of the blue. He was totally fed up with the Guzmán-Iglesias' marital conflicts and drunken fights. The day before his departure, he proposed to Elena, and she accepted. With their suitcases ready to go, they both handed over their keys to the owners. The Guzmán-Iglesias protested Elena's decision without prior notice.

"Go to the same hell where you came from! Take your keys and shut up, you devil's spawns!" Manuel yelled at them, fed up with all their stupidity.

Manuel and Elena grabbed their luggage and headed for the coast to take a boat to Puerto Rico. The twins could not say goodbye to them, mourning their departure privately, in the room that they both still shared by choice. Only Serena was able to go out and say goodbye to the newlyweds, despite the opposition of the owners of the house. As expected, she was the only person to hear from them once they settled in Ponce, six months after their departure. Serena wrote to them promising to visit them one day.

The nanny could not stop focusing on the increasing speed of the calendar; the days were rushing faster than greyhounds after the rabbit on the tracks. The twins had just turned five years old and she had spent months searching for the most suitable school for the girls. Serena, who was meticulous by nature, selected a private secular institution, in which the use of a uniform was not required. Yet, she believed that her choice would result in some kind of opposition on the part of the parents. However, after explaining her school preference, she was not surprised by their indifferent reaction. Regardless, she had expected at least some kind of opinion, given the nature of the matter. She would have liked them to assert themselves and tell her for once that they were indeed the girls' parents. Once again, not objecting to the slightest detail, nor any of her decisions, Serena had no option but to exhale. The disappointment of carrying all the weight on her shoulders never ceased to mortify her. Not only did she have to think of even the smallest detail about the lives of the girls, but she also had to witness the indifference of a couple that had been granted a purchased parental title. Once again, she rolled her usual monologue in her mind, as she went upstairs to her bedroom.

"It is obvious that I am their mom and dad. I never thought that by signing a simple nanny contract, I would inherit their full custody" the young woman voiced her complaint aloud, once in the silence of her bedroom, while attempting to shake off all the absurd, and oblivious behavior she often witnessed.

From that moment on, she would no longer bother to ask them anything else. The Guzmán-Iglesias couple seemed to navigate those waters way better. In the past, whenever Serena expected them to make decisions, she noticed how upset and indecisive they would get, and always avoided answering her questions. If she wanted to inform them of important details about the twins, they would both walk away immediately, saying that they had some sort of social commitment. It was in situations like those that Serena visualized herself as the house cat. The moment she showed up to discuss a concern, she would make all the rats and cockroaches living under the same roof, run in terror seeking protection.

The first day of school arrived too soon and Serena felt as though her brain discharged a growing level of electricity into her nervous system. She envisioned it as the heavy traffic of New York City, during rush hours. She felt the pressure of her heartbeat on the organ's neurons; their acceleration causing her an anxiety-ridden pain. Had she not known about such experience, she would have thought she was having a heart attack. Still, it was the stress created by all the responsibility she carried on her shoulders. She knew that any mistake in the girls' upbringing would be her fault and that whatever glory she prompted in the girls' lives was not hers, but instead Felipa's...and perhaps... Rogelio's. She was the taxpayer and they were the recipients of the profits. Based on that silent reality, she was extremely careful about all the decisions she made.

That first school morning, she woke the girls up. She had them perform their early hour grooming routine, and then, she dressed them according to their preference. As usual, if she deemed the clothes were not acceptable or appropriate for the occasion, Serena persuaded them to decide on another clothing item. They rarely complained, aware that she was their loving and reasonable *mother for hire*. They even called her mommy when only the three of them were together. Serena had explained to them that they should never address her that way in front of anyone, because if they did, they could lose her forever. It was more than obvious that Felipa would not tolerate it. Despite not investing time in them, just knowing that she contributed financially to their upbringing and that her signature appeared on the adoption contract, she was the ruling sovereign in her kingdom. Fearing parting ways with the only adult they deeply loved, the twins never violated their silent agreement.

Days before taking the twins to school for the first time, Serena had received the first letter from Manuel and Elena. The nanny was glad to hear the good news from her friends about a better job and their new home. Despite her joy, she did not share the news with the girls to avoid getting them sad just before starting their school life. As it was, Serena was already antsy about it. She prayed for her classmates to accept them, and to never find out about their unusual circumstances. The nanny was also very nervous about the peculiarities of their character. Not only were they intense in the way they looked at things, but they had also reached an extraordinary maturity in their short lives. Their nanny believed that they were very special and even more beautiful than the huge sunflowers that grow in the open meadows. Thinking about them in her nervous state, she found a certain level of reassurance in a swift thought that entered her mind. It was her sudden realization that her emotions were as disoriented as a meteorite lost in the night about to collide and breakdown.

"What a fool I am! Children today are not like we were. They are just like my girls, but without the dragonflies" she thought.

Without pondering on anything else, the three of them arrived at school, transported by Carlos. He got out of the car and helped the girls with their backpacks. Serena and the twins approached the school gates. They had requested Serena to be allowed to enter by themselves. She agreed and only watched them cross the school yard into the building, as she walked back to the car. She observed that the first contact with their classmates had been positive. Feeling released from an obviously unfounded concern, she raised her gaze to the sky to thank the higher powers.

Apart from the pleasure that education brought them, being in school was a sheltering experience for them. However, they remained very independent, seldom seeking or claiming anything from anyone. Their peers liked them and felt a particular attraction to them. Although they wondered on occasion about their excessive clothing, they never asked them about it. Throughout their school-life their classmates simply viewed them as human riddles. They would secretly analyze them without the girls knowing it, or so they thought. The twins always knew when their classmates observed them closely because they could feel the rising temperature on the side of the face they would be observing. Sometimes they felt heat on both sides of their faces, and some others, all around the head, making them feel like they had a fever. However, feeling hot was always very pleasant to them. Accustomed to being observed as thought they were lab specimens they were not disturbed by the stares.

When they observed Silvana, a little more introverted and with a fluctuating expression, they saw the depths of an abyss in her shinny dark obsidian eyes. At other times, they seemed to reveal a somewhat firm character, and a mystery akin to nature's underground caves. Yet, in a matter of seconds, they could perceive a changing fluidity, as if her nature were like the planet's tectonic plates responding to its own whim.

When analyzing Marina, they looked into her olive-colored eyes, and they could see the infinite depth of the lonely forests, where the birds listen to themselves and waters flow without barriers. They saw the movement of the wind caught between the trees and the smooth flight of swallows. Sometimes they could hear her when she softly imitated the sounds of birds. Other times, they watched her move her hands up and down, as if she were a butterfly. Whenever she engaged in these activities, she seemed to be in an altered state as if she were in a hypnotic trance.

Regardless of the opinion their classmates would have about them, the twins never found out, nor did they care. They preferred the school situation instead of that of a house where the air was denser and more stifling with every passing day. The childish idea of believing the home scenes to be a live soap opera had vanished once they turned four. It was as though after having tasted the whiskey from the bottle, they realized that everything they had lived before, was only a theater of true absurdity. The only thing that was real and tangible for them was Serena, the dragonflies, and the field. The rest of their home life was like makeup. After a few hours, it fades showing the real face behind it. The misfortune of such insight was seeing how it continued to be applied every day, perhaps not out of desire, but out of habit.

In the blink of an eye, the sisters turned eighteen. Over the years, Serena never ceased to be mortified by the parents' disregard of their daughters' birthdays. Nonetheless, she expected that they at least acknowledged the importance of this particular birthday.

"How could they not…if it marked the beginning of their adult life?" she would repeat out loud in the privacy of her room, aware that it would not happen.

Just like the three of them always did, they celebrated the birthday wherever the twins decided. What Serena didn't know was that the parents never knew the twins' exact date of birth. Since they had not witnessed their delivery, they were always confused about the date. In reality, they never bothered to check their birth certificate. Their desire to know was always brief, and soon dismissed by any of their frivolous commitments. There was always a meaningless circumstance that took their minds off their flimsy intention of celebrating the girls' birthday. Even a trivial phone call could derail them from learning the real date. It was just another disregarded fact about them; a potential golden opportunity the couple never recorded in their shallow minds.

On the other hand, despite of having been very popular throughout their academic lives, the twins never had close friends, nor had they attended the activities to which they had been invited. It seemed natural to them to evade crowds in order to avoid compromising situations. It was inevitable not to consider a potential encounter with the dragonflies, which no one could have ever understood. The very thought of inadvertently exposing their secret, terrified them. Despite the risk, they already felt the desire to leave home to begin a new stage in their life.

Serena was very concerned when they spoke about it because she felt that she would lose them. In addition to that, she would experience the uncertainty of looking for a new home to help raise small children once again. It saddened her because she had been with the twins the longest, and her care had been way more personal than in any home she had been before. Nonetheless, before she could suffer and mourn the vicissitudes of an unwanted change, the twins asked her to leave home with them. Serena was relieved, but she had no idea how they intended to make such plan work. Still, the girls promised her to come up with the right solutions. Yet fate, often indifferent to human desires, took action on the matter. The Guzmán-Iglesias couple, always looking for the opportunity to appear in high society magazines, announced that they would take a trip on their yacht to their native island of

Puerto Rico. Then, on their way back home to Miami, they would also stop in the Dominican Republic.

The twins preferred not to go on the trip because they did not want to miss college classes to be at sea with them, and because they could not freely wear a bathing suit or shorts. Faced with the threat of Felipa Isabel to kick them out of the house, and create a full-blown scandal, they were forced to accompany their parents. Although they knew that both their contract parents would suffer the social consequences more than anyone, the thought of being the reason for her ill-minded humiliation, was overwhelming. Therefore, they agreed to go as long as Serena also went with the family. Felipa Isabel accepted immediately, because despite never having expressed her gratitude, she felt a lot of respect and admiration for the nanny. Whenever she thought about her, she always held her in high regards.

"She looks so much like him! She could have been my daughter." Felipa thought regarding Serena.

Felipa Isabel was a woman who kept painful secrets. She had never told anyone that after adopting the two girls and reading an incredible number of nannies' files, upon seeing Serena's photo, she instantly chose her. Her face reminded her of Salvador, the young man she loved the most in life. For several years he was her boyfriend in high school, until one day she became pregnant. When she told him, he ran like a terrified goose and she never knew of his whereabouts again. Amid tears and suffering that she did not confide to anyone, Felipa Isabel became very ill. Two months later, her body discarded the fetus, while she was sitting on the toilet. It was a traumatic and very distressing event for her. Her soul was as broken as an egg accidentally falling from the hands of a poultry farmer.

For about fifteen minutes she cried observing the fetus, not knowing what to do. She found herself dipping her hands into the bloody water to scoop it out for a careful bath in the sink. After drying it off, she sat on her bathroom floor, sobbing while holding her dead baby. Then, she hugged it gently. She couldn't help but wonder if it had been a girl or a boy. Not being able to tell, she called it Luna-Sol and kissed its disproportionate head and a face that had no defined features, except for a hint of eyes. She ran her hands gently over the little legs and arms that had already begun to grow. Almost half an hour later, she got up and took it to her room. She dressed it by covering its torso with a lilac and turquoise fabric, which she cut to suit the embryo. Then she lay on the bed cradling it on her bare chest for a long time. She caressed its little head gently, while she sang a song between sobs.

Then she accepted the inevitable. It was obvious to her that she had to bury the fetus. She released a sigh from deep within her soul, and feeling overwhelmed, she placed it on a little pillow she made. Without hardly realizing it, she had also prepared a tiny coffin out of a small wooden box, where she placed the cushion with the little body. She prayed while crying. She offered a prayer and a gesture of her tenderness to the delicate body, and then put a wooden cover on the coffin. She wrote the name Luna-Sol in ink, and then proceeded to bury it in her backyard. When she physically recovered, she bought an ornamental figure of a sun and moon and placed it on the grave. No one ever knew anything about her sorrow. She only told her mother that she had bought the statue for her favorite place in the courtyard, just because it was so beautiful.

Seven years later, she met Rogelio. She married him since both their families knew each other well. Yet, she never forgot the experience she had with Salvador. Throughout the years, her frozen trauma did not allow her to conceive, nor to tell her story to her husband. It was suppressed in her memories just like centuries erase most traces of ancient civilizations.

When Felipa Isabel looked at the twins, she wanted to be able to give them love and the best of herself. However, the silence and repression of so many years, had frozen her ability to show love. It had essentially been transformed into an inner distress that she did not recognize. The root of her tree of emotions, had been cut off by the fear and immaturity of a frightened young man. She found herself alone in the middle of the storm. The only thing he knew to do was to run away, unable to offer her at least a supporting umbrella. Then her damaged tree of emotions rotted to the point of losing trust in her ability to love and manifest it. In her frozen soul, any attempts at howling like an injured and angered wolf were muffled. Even the twins, whom she had visualized as a new opportunity at life before they arrived, seemed untouchable after they arrived. A transparent wall of fear always got in the way when contemplating to get close, or even wanting to kiss them. Within that tough wall of battered emotions, she could only remember the smallest coffin she had ever seen in her entire life.

Everyone, oblivious to the experience that had caused her such hiatus, believed that she was heartless, frivolous, and unpleasant. Unfortunately, she became that person others loved to share with, out of sheer interest. The twins had also always regarded her with indifference, as a stranger, since they never shared even a single moment of tenderness with her. As for Rogelio, he did what she asked him to do. He was a phantom father and husband, who needed a symbolic wife from the upper class, and who could show up with him to all his activities. And of course, she had to be a beautiful woman who enjoyed, as much as he did, the alcoholic drinks he produced. Felipa Isabel had all the qualities he had always wanted in a wife.

In short, for the repressed and frustrated woman, her life was a constant rainy day. She always thought about the same thing. Even during her trip to Puerto Rico, while enjoying the sun on the deck of her beautiful white yacht with mahogany wooden details, Felipa Isabel remembered a shadow. It was always an unclear thought of Luna-Sol. In the blink of a second, that remembrance would leave her mind as if it were smoke between her hands. She realized later, in a moment of wisdom, that she was torturing herself pointlessly over a distant past. Without further ado, she emptied her mind into the amphorae of the sea. Lying on her favorite lounge chair, and wearing her turquoise bikini to match the color of her eyes, she watched the twins in the distance. For the first time, she noticed that they were always fully dressed.

"Marina. Silvana. Come here, my daughters" she called them with a sweet tone in her voice that they had never heard before.

The girls looked at each other, appreciating the sincerity of her words, which created a tremendous confusion in their hearts. Serena also sensed a loving energy in the words that pierced her heart like a lightning jolt. Felipa Isabel felt awakened from her long-lasting nightmare. She called again, thinking that the wind had not allowed her grown daughters to hear her voice. The young women proceeded to walk towards her, displaying a remarkable curiosity in their eyes. Then Felipa addressed them, feeling that the soft and warm air of her Antillean country had softened her heart, with its generous and caring spirit. She felt love running through her veins again. She felt as though the ocean also supported her healing; imbibing her old emotional barrier with its salty gales. Everyone noticed a change of color in the air, but no one spoke about it, due to its strange and subtle nature. Felipa Isabel smiled with happiness, because in a single instant she had consolidated all her sorrow from the past. She realized the damage she had caused to those who lived with her. Seeing the young women come to her side, Felipa Isabel was saddened. With her eyes flooded with the raindrops of her regret, and a voice made of broken glass, she spoke to them.

"Do you know… my darlings? I feel like I was just born. I want you to forgive me for not giving you the attention and love you both deserved" she asked of them, allowing the buds of her affection to sprout for them, for the first time.

"Don't be sorry, mom. We forgive you" the twins told her in unison, as one after the other leaned over to hug her dearly. "Please, my daughters, learn to love me," she asked of them with a trembling voice.

"We never stopped loving you. We only respected your distance" Marina replied sweetly, while Silvana affirmed it with a gesture.

"I know you don't ever wear a bathing suit because of the dragonflies" Felipa Isabel told them.

"Who told you such a thing?" Silvana asked her.

"I saw you both with Serena in the field one day. I didn't want to startle you with my presence. The sad thing about all this, is that right at this moment is when I understand why you always wear so many clothes."

"We're used to it and we like it," Marina replied.

"Are you sure?"

"Yes I am."

"I am too" Silvana told her.

"Well then, I will be ok with it, but in front of me, you can let the dragonflies come. You know? When they told me, I thought it was just a folktale!"

Serena listened to Felipa Isabel and despite rejoicing at her sudden change, she felt jealous. Yet, she despised to be upset about it. She realized her own emotion was an act of unfounded selfishness. Although the girls thought that the sudden transformation of Felipa Isabel was wonderful, it did not cross their minds to prefer her over Serena. They looked at her from a distance and realized that Felipa's confession had been an unusual assault on Serena's motherly affections.

As they both approached her, they didn't need to ask any questions.

"I know I have no reason to feel this way. I'm such a fool! Actually, I just want to be very happy for you," Serena said.

The twins didn't reply. They just hugged her, and showing her all their tenderness, they reaffirmed their unconditional love for her. Serena offered them a broad smile, and once again, she felt comforted by all the love they always gave her. She let them know that a person who has felt a lot of pain in their heart, often tends to be callous toward others. She asked the twins to give Felipa some love in the future. The twins smiled, agreeing with Serena. However, they clearly expressed to Serena that she would always continue to be the first one in their hearts. She responded offering them her usual tender smile. She asked them not to ever worry about it again, telling them that her jealousy had been unfounded and short-lived, for she never doubted their love for her. Therefore, she asked them to spend some quality time with Felipa.

Upon reaching the port of San Juan Bautista, Felipa Isabel and the twins went shopping while visiting the beautiful colonial city. Serena used the opportunity to call Manuel and Elena to announce them of her arrival in Puerto Rico. She invited them to spend the day with her in San Juan. However, the couple insisted she and the twins should spend their vacations with them in the southern city of Ponce. That afternoon, Serena told the Guzmán-Iglesias that she would go to Ponce for about four days to visit her old friends, and then fly to Miami, to avoid obstructing their initial travel plans.

By the time Serena would return to San Juan, the Guzmán-Iglesias would have already set sail for the Dominican Republic. After Serena's chat with Felipa and Rogelio, the twins let Serena know that they wanted to go with her. Serena asked for Felipa's consent regarding the twins' traveling with her.

Felipa Isabel did not object to their going, but she did not agree to let them fly back to Miami from Puerto Rico.

The Guzmán-Iglesias' couple then decided to shorten their stay in San Juan and travel to the Dominican Republic for a few days. They would depart from the port of the colonial city to the west of the island, until they reached Santo Domingo. After a two-day stop in the Dominican capital, they would get Serena and the twins at the airport in Ponce. The entire family would then return to San Juan, skirting the south and east, towards the northern port. Then they would spend the rest of their vacations together in Puerto Rico. Although the changes in plans upset Felipa Isabel a lot, she wanted to give Serena and the twins the opportunity to visit those whom they had always remembered with great affection. She recognized that it was of particular interest to his daughters, because they had not been able to say goodbye to the couple they loved and never forgot. Then, Felipa felt sad for a few moments and asked Serena to apologize to them, on her behalf. The nanny replied that she would be happy to do so and also hinted that she could do it in person upon her return to Puerto Rico, once reaching the port of Ponce.

"I would like to, but I don't have the strength to face them. I can't do it! I need to have way more courage than I have now" Felipa Isabel told her, removing her thick blonde hair away from her cheeks.

"It's been thirteen years," Serena replied.

"…thirteen more can pass by. Don't you understand how slow everything moves in my soul? Fear and silence have always taken me hostage. I only promise to try, Serena."

The next morning, Serena and the twins were walking away with their luggage, to spend four days in Ponce. They had about three hours in San Juan before Manuel and Elena would to pick them up at the Plaza de San José. Delighted with their adventure, they went to have breakfast and visit the colonial city. They walked down Tetuán Street to Colón Square and then, to Norzagaray Street. They went down San José Street to the corner of Christ Street, to reach the Christ Chapel. On their way, they were able to appreciate the well-preserved beauty of the old forts, the city squares, the blue cobblestones, and the stunning Spanish colonial buildings. Meanwhile, the Guzmán-Iglesias couple sailed for the Dominican Republic, despite knowing that the weather would be bad in the Caribbean. It was August 29, 1979.

Once back at the Plaza de San José, Serena and the young women saw Manuel and Elena arrive in their car. They hugged one another happily, as if they had never stopped seeing each other. They boarded the car and headed south, crossing the belly of the majestic Cordillera

Central, the mountainous area of the island's interior, until they reached the Ciudad Señorial de Ponce. There, they visited some of the local mansions by carriage, the beautiful town square, and also the centuries old fire house, preserved since its construction in 1882, with its red and black colors. The visiting ladies and the couple, had a great time sharing with their longtime friends. All of them had taken vacations just to see each other and share their happiness together again.

However, fate had other plans. The next day, they had to stay inside the couple's house, as Hurricane David was passing about 70 miles south of Puerto Rico. With a simple blow, David had left twenty-one inches of water on the island of Hispaniola. That same afternoon, David became a category five hurricane. By August 31st, it was hitting the Dominican Republic, crossing the belly of the island like no other storm since 1930. It crossed through the capital, Santo Domingo, unleashing its wolfpack of howling winds. Giant trees were uprooted as though they were just plastic trees in an architectural model. Metal roofs flew aimlessly like silver kites. The Caribbean Sea, a subjugated accomplice of the nefarious David, lashed the coasts as if in rebellion, while the hard arm of the hurricane tore the green and generous body of Hispaniola.

Many missing people were swallowed by the elements. Some were hurled by the winds, and others were thrown away by rain and wind into the treetops, while others lay buried in the rubble. Before leaving the island, the hurricane unleashed all its rage on the Dominican Republic, stealing the lives of countless of her children. As a cruel and wrathful tyrant, it abandoned soil, only after causing suffering and misery. The hurricane had devastated the island with its stench of death; followed by the anguished cries of a people in agony. Before the news of the enormous destruction in the Dominican Republic, Serena had felt a strong twitching sensation in her large intestine, provoked by the dreaded intuition of the Guzmán-Iglesias' fate. She never imagined that she and the twins would be with Manuel and Elena awaiting the news that was never informed directly to them. Nonetheless, the local government reported that the coastal areas and the port were totally destroyed.

Thousands of people walked among the ruins, without food or water, without electricity or hope. The cries and complaints of the entire population were magnified in the air like the deafening songs of cicadas. From one coast to the other, everything was devastation. The sad faces of the survivors were distorted by grief. The eyes of children and adults showed the shocking pain of their souls' profound affliction. Many of the little ones stopped talking, frozen like statues, in the face of the never-before-experienced trauma. It was as if the devil himself had shown up for a few hours to rob them of their happiness. Confronted with the apocalyptic scenario, it was evident that the Guzmán-Iglesias' yacht had vanished with the destruction of the port and the rest of the vessels.

The devouring whirlwind had mercilessly swallowed Felipa Isabel and Rogelio, like everyone else in its path. The Guzmán-Iglesias twins needed to release their grief, and they asked Serena to speak with Manuel and Elena to allow them to spend the night on the roof of their house. They agreed to the request and provided the twins with two floating beach beds. Under the bright moonlight, they took off their clothes and laid down on the cots. They welcomed their friends, the dragonflies, to purge their guilt and grief. This way they could start healing from the deep torture of knowing that they were accomplices in two homicides, planned by fate at their expense. Had they not wanted to visit their friends Manuel and Elena, Felipa Isabel and Rogelio would have stayed with them in San Juan, according to their original schedule. It was painful to realize that they would never feel the tenderness their mother had just liberated from the chains that bound her heart. As for their father, he always followed Felipa Isabel's lead. Therefore, they would not exactly know how Rogelio would have adjusted his behavior to harmonize with that of his wife. However, he certainly would have found the way just to please her.

The sisters could only hand over all burden of their profound regret, to their aerial friends. Yet, they were aware that in life there are always issues that take longer time to resolve. As expected, the minute they lay naked, the dragonflies arrived. The winged creatures shone in the moonlight, like those 1960's four-colored wheel projectors do on the silver manmade Christmas trees. The sisters spent the entire night under the healing influence of the spell of the little flying magicians, whose translucent wings vibrated to create a therapeutic veil for them.

Before dawn, the twins entered Manuel's and Elena's house. Marina and Silvana had lost their desire to stay in Ponce, preferring the solitude of a hotel room in San Juan. They both implored Serena to return to the capital. In unknown ways, they feared that if their parents came back and couldn't find them, they would leave forever. Listening to their words of denial, Serena only replied that their parents would know where to find them.

"They can't get here anymore, Serena. Can't you see that their yacht was wrecked? Please, tell her, Silvana!" Marina implored her sister.

"I agree with Marina, Serena. They would arrive in San Juan" Silvana responded.

Serena had to explain to them the fact that, during hurricanes, there are usually no inbound or outbound trips. She clarified that any plane or boat coming in or leaving, would do so to transport vital emergency supplies to help the victims. Still, the twins insisted on returning to San Juan to manifest their sadness in solitude. That explanation seemed reasonable to Serena.

She perfectly understood the twins' wish. However, she felt it was a shame to leave after waiting so long to see her friends. While they all shared Serena's feelings, they also understood that many a times situations don't happen as anticipated. Therefore, they were grateful to have shared with the couple at least for one day. Even those very brief hours of memories would last a lifetime. Serena, Manuel and Elena looked at each other sadly, but they understood that sometimes a minute can be more valuable than a year.

"This is where the importance of the content of time lies" Serena concluded after reconsidering her initial view of the events. Thus, in a tight embrace of five souls, they said their goodbyes, hoping to meet again sometime soon.

Serena and the twins left that same morning for Old San Juan. They settled in the beautiful colonial hotel, located few blocks away from the Christ Chapel. As soon as they arrived, Marina went down by herself to walk towards the *Parque de las Palomas* (Pigeons' Park). She sat on a bench to observe the birds that perched on the children, especially on those who offered them food. She was so enthralled with the chirping of pigeons, that without realizing it, she began to coo as if the sound of the flying creatures had mesmerized her. An older man of about seventy-seven years old, had been watching her for over five minutes. Noticing that she was in a trance, he asked her if she was alright. When she didn't respond, he kept on calling on her until he got her to react.

"Did you call me or did I imagine it?" Marina asked Don Fernando.

"It was hard for me to get you to respond," said the elderly man.

"I was just looking at the pigeons."

"You did a lot more than that, young lady. You were cooing just like them."

Marina explained to him that she rid her heart of all pain when she felt in communion with any sublime kind of flying creature. She told him that she always felt like family to everything that flies; and also told him that her fairy godmothers were not birds, but dragonflies. The man smiled at her and replied that he also visited the park to see the pigeons. Upon hearing his response, Marina asked him to tell her his name, and he replied that it was Fernando.

"I'm Marina. I'll be back in a month, or maybe in three years. Either way, I'll come back here to talk to you. Take good care of yourself!" she told him as she waved goodbye to the octogenarian.

Marina got up and walked away towards the hotel, without looking back. Upon her arrival, she climbed the stairs and watched the sculptures on the courtyard. She walked to the bar and sat down. Then, she ordered a shot of whiskey like the ones his parents used to drink. Upon receiving it, she raised it up high and, staring up into the sky, she made a toast for her deceased parents. Then she drank it all in one gulp and headed for her bedroom. People stared at her with a certain level of confusion, as is usually the case when someone yells words out of context in a crowd.

When she got to the room, she found Serena and Silvana having lunch. Her sister looked at her with some distaste and asked her if she had been drinking whiskey. When she answered yes with a gesture, Silvana reproached her for drowning her sadness just like Felipa Isabel used to do. Marina showed that she agreed with her sister, through her facial expression. She then realized that Serena was trying to conceal she had been crying, and Marina couldn't help but to feel bad about her drinking. She sat next to Serena and hugged her, asking for her forgiveness. She explained to her that she was only grieving, because the news of their parents' death, no matter how indifferent they were, was still a nightmare. She imagined that the news might have already spread through all the media in Latin America. So, she preferred not to watch television, nor listen to the radio; or see a newspaper or a magazine.

Silvana confirmed that they had seen the news on TV. They had announced that both parents were presumed to have passed away and that their bodies might never be recovered. They had found the port entry documentation and also some of the remains of the yacht. At that point Serena told them that it was better to return to Miami.

✱✱✱

The sisters were legal heirs to all of their parents' properties and businesses. Their Miami mansion continued to be their residence, even though Marina insisted on moving to San Juan. However, both Silvana and Serena managed to persuade her to stay in Miami and finish the college degree she had begun in August 1978. For Silvana it was important to stay in the city, as she was interested in taking over the reins of her parents' businesses. She had already started to pave her way towards accomplishing that goal when she enrolled in college for a business administration degree. Meanwhile, Marina had joined the arts and literature program, and was certainly not interested in being in charge of any business. However, she had only shown interest in consuming the spirits of the family distillery.

During her second year of university studies, Silvana fell in love with the eldest son of a prominent family with whom she shared the affinity of her career. However, they both feared that their family would oppose their relationship for a simple reason. She was one of the twins born in Mexico, adopted through Guzmán-Iglesias family contacts. For William such detail was unimportant. Yet,

Silvana worried that his parents, just like many other people of higher birth, her ancestry would probably be unacceptable to their social stature. When the relationship crystallized in the early 1980s, William proposed to Silvana. His plans were to wait to graduate in May 1982 and get married in June. Serena was more than happy with the courtship, as she considered William the perfect candidate for Silvana. However, Marina recognized that this event would mark her sister's separation from her. She just hoped that he would be a good husband and an ideal companion for Silvana. After all, she had decided to settle in San Juan, and leave behind the social impositions of her family's status and position. The announcement of the wedding only hastened the moment of Marina's departure.

It was common knowledge between the sisters and Serena that Marina would move to Puerto Rico immediately after the wedding; provided the bride and groom were able to resolve their family differences. She was aware that for several months there was some tension and opposition from William's parents.

Although the Stewarts seemed to have agreed to their son's wedding, the silent *cold war* from William's parents, was a constant battle that continued at home. As a result, he was privately growing angrier and overwhelmed, while he allowed Silvana to continue with the wedding plans. William got to a point where he felt he was failing his fiancée. Before talking to her about his inner turmoil, he notified his parents that he would cancel the wedding. However, in return, he would move to Denmark for the rest of his life. In doing so, he would never come back to Florida to visit anyone, nor would he speak to his parents ever again. He informed them emphatically that moving away was his alternate option. After a couple of days of pondering about the best family resolution, his parents concluded that they could learn to love their future daughter in law. Due to their son's anger at their prejudice, the Stewarts realized that their inflexible stance on the wedding reflected poorly on them. Regardless of being adopted daughters, Silvana and her sister were heirs to one of the largest fortunes in the state. Therefore, they concluded that their origin should not have mattered to them. Then, they spoke to their son, and asked him to forgive and forget their inflexible behavior.

All along, Marina could sense that her sister's in-laws were troubled by her background. There were instances in which she would notice the subtle nuances of their discomfort, as well as the practiced facade used to cover their deficiencies. Yet, she never mentioned anything to her sister.

"Instead of appreciating the beauty of the wonderful adopted *mestiza*, it was the allure of her wealth that finally won them over," Marina thought as she was informed that there was no disapproval to the couple's wedding. However, Marina did not comment anything to Serena or to her sister. She only hoped that Silvana would keep her last name. It would be a way to honor the couple who rescued them. Marina thought they deserved such distinction despite them having lived most of their lives entangled in the corridors of their personal madness.

The fact that Felipa Isabel realized her mistakes as a mother before she died had changed history for Marina. She wanted to preserve that fortuitous treasure through their surnames. When commenting to her sister over her concern, Silvana reassured her that keeping her surnames was not negotiable. William knew very well that their companies were named after their parents and that it was logical for both heiresses to continue with the tradition. With that response, Marina gently accepted their marriage, and the sisters' parted ways as a natural part of their lives.

The little family of three was preparing for their change of scenery. As a result of their future physical detachment, the dragonflies that caressed the twins when surrendering to the elements, would not be the same, although they would have the same purpose. At the moment, Serena and the two sisters were in charge of maintaining the mansion, and when they could no longer do it, they hired help through an agency. They had only a driver as a full-time employee, but they had no maid, no cook, and no butler. Inside the house, only the three of them lived, as mother and daughters. Thus, the days continued passing by very fast, but without setbacks or disconcerting stumbles.

However, just six months before the wedding, an unknown and unexpected man knocked on the door. Marina opened, without releasing the chain from the upper bolt. She looked at him suspiciously because she had the intuition that he was a shady man, perhaps a conman or hustler looking for trouble.

"Good morning, what brings you here?" Marina asked.

"A very important matter" the man replied.

"Just tell me from out there."

"You are Marina, aren't you?"

"Who is asking?"

"Your father, Luis Segarra."

"I'm sorry, you're in the wrong house. I don't think my father was a Spaniard. He was Mexican. Have a good day!" she said after recognizing the Iberian Spanish accent.

As Marina attempted to close the door, Luis squeezed his hand in to stop it from closing. Serena had overheard the conversation, and became speechless, nervous, pale, and paralyzed. Silvana, who was walking behind Serena, saw her and asked her what was wrong. Marina turned around when she heard her sister's questioning. She noticed Serena's stunned face and inquired about the veracity of the man's words. The nanny took a breath, shaking her head up and down, while a stream of tears ran down her cheeks. Immediately observing her gesture of affirmation, Marina opened the door. She looked at him apprehensively, from head to toe, with a stern expression. Then she allowed him to enter, while asking him the reason of his unexpected intrusion in their lives. Silvana looked at her with confusion and asked her why she had allowed him to enter.

"Why do you think? ... So that you and I could see for once, he who claims to be our biological father…displaying a false accent" said Marina to Silvana.

"I am a Spaniard, but I lived in Mexico for many years. All of you can say whatever you want about me. Your mother Soledad was young and I left her. When I returned to her and asked to be forgiven, she no longer wanted me in her life" Luis told them.

"Then, we don't want you either. I can only imagine she got rid of you because you either abused her or you were a womanizer…maybe both" Marina replied.

"I wasn't the best of husbands, Marina, but I've tried to find you both for too long. I came to Miami two years ago, because I learned you were here. I did not want to introduce myself to you without settling first. Now that I am, I felt ready to meet the both of you."

The twins looked at each other, and immediately knew their answer to him. Silvana embraced Serena in her arms and very politely told him that it was a pleasure to have met him. However, she asked him to leave and never come back. She explained that while they had nothing against him, he shouldn't expect them to open their arms to him either. After Silvana spoke, Marina made clear that his time had passed when he abandoned their biological mother. Although Luis Segarra acknowledged his shortcomings as a younger man, he begged his daughters to let him tell them the full story of their marriage, as they did not know what had happened during the years that came after. Despite his plea, they wanted nothing from him, and decided to ask him to leave and never return.

Luis left crestfallen, understanding that his presence in his daughters' lives was unwanted. As the door closed behind him, Serena sat on the sofa, while the twins looked at her, expecting an answer. She cried as she told them that Felipa had forbidden her to tell them anything she knew. Then, Silvana looked at her, while she mouthed some slightly reproaching words.

"We would have never said anything to Felipa, Mother." You have known that since forever. I know you always have legitimate reasons, but why didn't you share important information about our origins? We had the right to know."

Although Serena recognized that Silvana was right, she explained that Felipa had the power to be very forceful when threatening. Serena explained that had the twins seen her face and body language, they would have also been shaken by terror. She told them that she looked like she had come from hell itself. Felipa was drunk and threatened to chop Serena into steaks, and feed her to the dogs. Serena realized that her boss was more than capable of taking her to the slaughterhouse when she was drunk. Silvana did not press Serena any further regarding her silence, remembering her mother's ill temper. While the twins had witnessed many marital fights, they had never heard either spouse threatening to kill one another. Yet, they could understand that Felipa would be occasionally cruel to an employee, considering that she would often feel superior just because of her position.

The twins realized that Serena knew very little about the Segarra. In short, they did not hear from Luis for a long time. However, the curiosity to know more remained latent in the mind of the twins, despite having sent him away without any hope of reconciliation. After they had asked him to never return, they knew there was a story he had wanted to share with the twins. Just like the waves of the sea wash off the shore, the twins eventually decided to erase Luis' fortuitous visit from their minds.

Silvana's nuptials were only a few months away. Therefore, the bride and groom hired a wedding planner to organize a party in style. That was the groom's parents' expectations. Silvana had actually preferred a simple and beautiful wedding, but decided not to antagonize her future in-laws. As it was, she felt lucky William had no issue with her secret, which he promised to never reveal to his parents. Without him knowing it, William's parents even commented among themselves that it was an excellent family strategy to introduce their other son to Marina. They left it as a possible silent alternative.

Those few months before her wedding were very difficult for Silvana. Not only was she finishing her studies, she was also graduating. Meanwhile, she worked in her company, while learning the business. Aware of her burden, Marina took control of the wedding preparations to give her sister a breather. She was in charge of informing the organizer of Silvana's preferences, even without having discussed them with her sister. Although Marina was also about to graduate, she had studied all summers, to have fewer requirements on her last semester. Therefore, she had quite a few hours available, not only to help with the wedding preparations, but also to learn the duties of the business, just in the event she decided to work at the company in the future.

In the blink of an eye, the wedding day had arrived. Marina had supervised all the details so that Silvana had a beautiful ceremony and a wonderful party. Since Silvana had wanted to get married at home, Marina managed to secure the priest of the church Silvana attended. He was scheduled to perform the nightly nuptial ceremony in the Guzmán-Iglesias' forest. A team of thirty people had adorned the trees with lightbulb vines, snaking then through the branches. As the wedding had fallen on a moonless night, Marina had anticipated that the lights would create a mysterious and magical glow.

The religious ceremony was held in the middle of the forest on a huge terrace connected to an ornamental flagstone path that led the way for the guests. The trail wound through the greenery, from the magnificent terrace at the back of the mansion, to the splendid plaza in the heart of the forest. Undulating silken translucent ribbons on both sides of the path, outlined the stroll of the bride dressed in a white lace gown, embroidered with pearls and diamonds.

Silvana walked wearing her long tulle veil. It seemed to fly like a thin vaporous wave between the two rows of ecclesiastical seats that her sister had managed to rent for her nuptial. They took up three-quarters of the terrace and accommodated all 150 guests. At the front, on a wooden platform, the workers had managed to create a temporary altar for the priest to carry out the ceremony. William awaited his bride right there, looking for her among the trees, while a soprano sang Bach's Ave Maria. Meanwhile, the bridesmaids headed by Marina, arrived at the altar, waiting for the bride. As Silvana entered from the forest, the guests threw orange blossom petals; their sweet citrusy aroma creating a sublime and magical atmosphere. Serena, sitting on the first bench, drowned in the depths of the spring that gushed from her eyes.

After the ceremony, dinner was served on the terrace of the mansion. William's parents hugged their daughter-in-law and took advantage of Marina's closeness to introduce her to Lawrence, their youngest son. After an emotional toast given by Serena, the bride and groom cut the cake, and afterwards, the newlyweds and their guests danced for several hours. Lawrence, unaware of her parents' intentions, invited Marina to dance. She agreed and after one dance and another, she also accepted an invitation to have dinner the next day. All the guests were wrapped up in the joy of the celebration. Then, like the passing of a flock of storks in the night, the newlyweds escaped without warning. José Manuel, the mansion's driver, awaited to take them to the airport on their way to Japan, where they would spend their honeymoon week.

Next morning, after finishing the last chores of the wedding and having drank so much, Marina went to bed exhausted. She slept for long hours and woke up the next day, around three in the afternoon. She showered and got ready for José Manuel to take her with Serena to the movies. In her absence, a work team was in charge of removing everything related to the celebration of the nuptials. Due to her heavy alcohol consumption, Marina never remembered having agreed to a date with her brother-in-law's brother, or even having met him.

The young man came looking for her. However, when he rang the doorbell, there was no one available to answer. With no one at the house at the moment, his repeated ringing of the bell went completely unnoticed. The only employees on the grounds were in the forest, complying with the cleaning requirements. There were also those of the contracted services, collecting seats, tables, and all the other articles pertinent to the celebration. After being stood-up, Lawrence decided not to return to Marina's mansion.

While the newlyweds were away on their honeymoon, Serena and Marina planned to empty Felipa Isabel's and Rogelio's suite to prepare it for the young couple. It seemed the most logical thing to do since it was the largest and most comfortable bedroom in the whole house. Besides, it was the most private, being apart from the other seven bedrooms of the mansion. They decided to get rid of all the personal items that reminded them of Felipa Isabel and Rogelio. To clear the furniture from the room, they had contacted a charity that would be in charge of donating all the pieces. They had also decided to hire a decorating firm to give the bedroom a new look and to modernize the windows, bathroom, and fixtures in the room.

Meanwhile, Serena and Marina estimated that in a single day they could collect and dispose of all unnecessary items before the builders and decorators arrived. They would only keep some things for sentimental reasons. Two days after the party, both began to work early, like industrious bees that achieve the best of the hives. In a synchronized way they emptied drawers, wardrobes and trunks; classifying their contents according to their value or importance.

"Mom, leave the hard work to me and just stay here in my company. I don't want you to get tired," Marina said to Serena.

"Don't you start with that again. Silvana has already given me an earful," Serena responded.

"You know she's right."

"All that nonsense the doctors say, is what makes me tired."

"My goodness! How stubborn can you be? What they tell you is not nonsense. Please, don't argue with me anymore."

"Very well, I won't, but I must do something," Serena answered Marina, quite annoyed.

"Well, go ahead, but I just want you to not overdo it. That's all."

They continued to remove things. Marina kept an eye on Serena as she sped up her participation in rearranging and cleaning. Serena could tell that Marina observed her whenever she would put forth more effort in working. Then, Marina asked Serena to focus her energies on discarding letters, outdated documents, and unimportant files. Serena agreed to do so aware that Marina was concerned about her well-being. After two hours of hard work, Marina found in the deepest place area of Felipa Isabel's closet, a small trunk with a padlock. She knew immediately that the content had to be of sentimental value just because it was too well hidden. Therefore, she picked it up and decided to search for the key. She intuited she would find it in the vanity where Felipa used to put her jewelry, makeup, and other everyday items. Toward the back of the second drawer, she found a small porcelain chest. She opened it sensing that Felipa Isabel would have put it there, just because she would have done the same.

She took the key and sat on the bed to open the box. With a single turn of the lock, she unleashed a door to another time in history. The ghosts of Felipa Isabel's parents came out, as well as the fallen leaves of her upbringing as a rich and lonely girl. Above all, the buried secret of a woman on pause, emerged from the grave as a profoundly held exhalation. Marina read the yellowish pages written on Luna-Sol, and she could feel Felipa's deep and lost love's heartache spiraling down. She pictured her mother's heart as a fragile bottle full of marbles, abruptly thrown from up high into the void. She could see it crash; its colored pieces scattered in all directions. Sobbing, she called Serena and asked her to read the page she pointed at while holding the diary. Serena took the journal from Marina's hands and sat next to her to read the passage.

"Poor Felipa!" She had no one to trust" Serena told her.

"Perhaps she feared the punishment of her parents."

They both looked at each other and Serena sadly expressed that it was terrible for many women to get pregnant and not be married. For many of their parents, it was like committing a terrible crime. Serena raised her eyebrows, while letting out a sorrowful sigh as she verbalized her thoughts to Marina. She remembered that as she grew up, women had always been upheld to higher moral standards than men. Even in clothing, in the house and in all places, the demands were remarkable. As she pondered on her unshared secrets, she could feel her throat constricting. She felt the burning liquid of her own suppressed tears. She then looked at the photo of Felipa on the dresser.

"How hard we had to be with ourselves. Silence hurt us a lot, but talking could have cost us our lives" she spoke to her in her thoughts.

Meanwhile, Marina tried to contain the river that flowed through her eyes. She stood up and went to the bar. She poured two glasses of whiskey, one for herself and one for Serena. Marina understood in that instant why Felipa drank so much. However, it was also obvious to her that there were also some other kinds of expectations for men. Perhaps not being able to fulfill societal and family's expectations, created a sense of guilt in many. While she didn't know much about Rogelio, just like Felipa, he drowned himself almost daily in a gold-filled alcoholic tank. Leaving her thoughts behind, Marina raised her shoulders and began to enjoy her favorite liquor. Returning to the room, she offered one of the glasses to Serena. To her surprise, she accepted it gladly.

"I'm going to drink it, and I dedicate it today to Felipa Isabel Iglesias" Serena said, raising her glass.

Marina smiled at her when she saw her so relaxed, because it was not her usual self. She took advantage of the occasion to ask her if she agreed that all men were scoundrels. Serena smiled and replied that scoundrels come in both sexes. She then said that the noun applied more often to some men; traditionally those who are prone to engaging in violent behaviors. Those men tend to take advantage of women because they're physically stronger. Then, Serena emphasized that those violent and disrespectful men need to learn to respect and love women, for it was women who gave them life. Then after a long sigh, Serena stated that all women in the world should be fully free to decide any aspect of life on their own. Marina just listened to her unusual conversation.

Upon returning from their honeymoon in Japan, Silvana and William would have their marital room already settled in the Guzmán-Iglesias' mansion. Silvana and William had agreed to live there before getting married, as she preferred that Serena not remain alone. In the past two years, the sisters had seen her health decline, although she insisted it was only momentary tiredness. However, Serena began to look very deteriorated after the wedding, which sparked a new conversation between the sisters, upon Silvana's return. As a result of the discussion, they decided to hire a maid and a cook. It was evident that none of the inhabitants of the mansion would have time to do housework. It was the twins' wish that Serena only rested and that José

Manuel, the driver, would always be available to drive her wherever she wanted.

Marina was ready to move to Puerto Rico even though she was concerned about Serena's health. However, she wanted to fulfill the deep desire that she had nurtured for several years. It had already been four days since Silvana arrived, and William would soon be officially settling into the residence. Therefore, Marina already had her luggage ready for leaving in the morning of the fifth day. Despite being saddened by Marina's departure, Serena and Silvana decided not to show their sorrow. Crying would only make her parting more difficult. Serena and the twins just held each other tightly in a three-way hug. As she got into the car, Marina reminded them to keep an eye on Luis Segarra, because she had the feeling that he would be lurking around.

On the way to the airport, she spent the entire trip making harmonious sounds she had learned from all kinds of birds. She made them as softly as she could to avoid José Manuel's attention. Yet, he listened silently for about ten minutes.

"Where did you learn to imitate so many birds?" he interrupted out of curiosity.

"It's something I've done since I was little, because it helps me relax."

"It's actually very soothing. What a great idea" he said smiling at her from the driver's mirror.

***

Marina arrived in San Juan in the afternoon and went to the furnished apartment that she had procured as a residence while in Miami. It was on the second floor of a building located in the highest part of Calle Cruz in Old San Juan. From her colonial balcony with its two traditional huge wooden doors, she could see the Atlantic Ocean in its airy elegance. Once established, every time she opened the doors, the mischievous wind blowing from the bay knocked the vase off her dining room table. Then it would exit through the twin kitchen doors on its journey to other areas of Old San Juan. To prevent the vase from breaking, Marina decided to fill it in with some heavy ornamental stones. Then, she could enjoy without any hesitation the aggressive circulation of the salty air, which moistened the high walls of her apartment.

Within days of her moving in, Marina met her immediate neighbor on the second floor of the adjoining building. She was a heavyset lady of about fifty-eight years of age, named Ms. Marta. She was a woman whose passions were like the tides of the ocean. She was moody, and she could be very sweet and affectionate at times, and at others, abrasive and hostile. Right off the bat, Marina sensed these changes and just by looking at her, she could tell if she was happy or upset. While she initially had some brief conversations with Marta, she soon remembered the lean, elderly man she had met at the Pigeons' Park. Without any hesitation, she decided to walk towards the Chapel of Christ to sit in the adjacent park and enjoy the constant presence of the birds. Shortly after her arrival in the park, she saw Mr. Fernando, the thin old man with a mustache and hair so white, it reminded her of the shiny color of the full moon. Then they both caught sight of each other.

"Do you remember me?" she said with a smile.

"How can I not remember you if you hum like a dove? Besides, you promised to come back and here you are" Don Fernando answered, very pleased to see her.

"Friends?" she asked him.

"Well, yes, just like grandfather and granddaughter. If my age doesn't bother you, yours doesn't bother me either. Do you want to have some fun?"

"I'm all ears. What do you propose?" she asked curiously.

Don Fernando often enjoyed to bless people at random, or things that crossed his path. After telling Marina, she became curious and agreed to join him. He opened his leather bag and showed her his cleaning items. Then, both went out into the neighborhood rubbing with cotton and alcohol all withering trees, damaged cars, rusty trash cans and any other objects he considered to be in a poor condition. Marina observed his actions with a lot of curiosity. She walked behind him, helping him occasionally and at other times, just observing his methodic action. They were walking along San Francisco Street, when she noticed him becoming particularly curious about some figurines that emulated a Spanish village, that could be seen from the threshold of a porcelain decor store. He pulled out another cotton ball from his leather bag, and soaked it with alcohol. Then, he walked up to the figurines and began to rub them, while telling Marina that the entire small town needed healing. A little worried, Marina replied that it was better for them to leave and avoid being escorted out of the store.

Don Fernando smiled while insisting that everyone could always benefit from a good blessing. Marina became nervous when she saw the owner approaching them, only to feel reassured when she realized that both men knew each other. The middle-aged man asked Don Fernando how many blessings did he need to bestow upon the villagers. He hinted that perhaps all the alcohol he had been putting on the figurines in previous occasions, might tarnish them.

The owner also reminded him that everything in his store had already been blessed by him several times. Don Fernando smiled and then said goodbye to the owner. Marina let the man know that she was just there to observe Don Fernando's blessings for the first time. Then she bid him farewell and left. Marina followed the old man as he continued his walk of consecrations.

A few minutes later, Don Fernando saw that a woman, looking for a notebook in her purse, dropped a wallet that ejected a wad of money. He walked over to the lady and he grabbed both, the wallet and the money, from the ground. He was in the process of anointing both before handing them over to the woman. Marina recognized that the woman was her neighbor. Before she could tell her about her money, Marta attacked Don Fernando.

"What are you doing, old troublemaker? Are you crazy?" the woman yelled at him.

"Enough is enough, Doña Marta! Do you want me to call the police about your abuse to a senior citizen? Don't you see that Don Fernando wants to give you the money that you just dropped on the ground? Let's clarify who the troublemaker is. Another person would have grabbed the money and left without you even realizing it" Marina said angrily.

Doña Marta took the money from Don Fernando's hands and left the moment he started to swab her with his alcohol. The old man looked at Marina and then, he let her know that he gave the sick woman some healing. Marina breathed in and smiled at him. Then she told him that, apparently, he could cause quite a lot of trouble with *those games* that others did not understand. Marina stated jokingly that she couldn't imagine how he had been able to make it to such an advanced age with his behavior. Don Fernando laughed mischievously as if he had been tickled. However, he offered her no response.

Before saying goodbye to her octogenarian friend, Marina thought she should take a trip to the mountains. She told Don Fernando that she would see him in two or three weeks, after she did some exploring. He offered to accompany her, but she did not accept because she did not know if Don Fernando had someone looking after him. However, she promised to see him again as soon as she returned. When Marina went back to her apartment, she saw Doña Marta sitting in her balcony. They both glanced at each other. Marina made it a point to look at her reproachfully. Since the first time they met, she became aware that her neighbor's behavior fluctuated from one moment to the next just like the tides do. However, after beating Don Fernando and not apologizing to him, once she was made aware of the truth, Marina felt disgusted at her ugly behavior. She wondered if she was really ugly because of her nasty expression, or if she was ugly because of her unpleasant personality. She decided to ignore those thoughts and not comment on anything. She realized that asking would be an impertinence of hers, since she herself had been the victim of inappropriate questions. She had sometimes heard people ask her, for no reason at all, if she was mentally ill. Therefore, she decided that it was better not to judge her neighbor, although she was upset at her for hitting Don Fernando. Without further thought, she began to speak to Marta.

"Good morning, Doña Marta."

"What do you want now?" Marta replied still angry.

"Why are you so hostile?" Marina asked her.

"Don't pretend that man didn't want to steal my money! You were just covering up for him, which means you tried to rob me too."

"I see. You don't think you dropped the money. I'm sorry you believe that. It's obvious that we can't be friends, but rest assured that I don't need your money. Have a nice day, ma'am. What a shame to be your neighbor!" Marina said feeling hurt.

Marina quickly entered her apartment and closed, in broad daylight, the balcony's imposing colonial doors. At that very moment she packed her suitcase and called a taxi. She asked the driver to take her to a particular car dealership, where she made a cash payment on a mountain-green all-terrain vehicle. After the purchase was finalized, she headed out with her map to the splendid Central Mountain Range. She crossed the mountainous body of the island until she reached Jayuya, a town in the coffee growing area, north of Ponce, the main city in the south. After passing through town, she noticed a sign at a farm, posting a coffee picking position. She stopped and walked to the main house on the ranch, and knocked on the door. Doña Isabel, the owner of the house who was a lady of about fifty years of age, opened the door. Marina looked at her and she thought the lady was perfect. According to her analysis, not only was she nice, she was also beautiful. Her only defect was one somewhat damaged front tooth. She couldn't understand why that tooth reminded her of Doña Marta. She could've sworn she saw it move and dance as if it had a personality of its own. Although the tooth's appearance puzzled her, she tried to prevent the lady from noticing her persistent observation. Inevitably, Doña Isabel was well aware, but did not comment on it, since she liked

Marina very much as well. Having both clicked with each other, the young woman let Isabel know that she was interested in the job.

"Are you sure? You don't seem to have sunbathed a single day in your life. Just looking at your shiny black hair and silky skin, I know this job isn't for you" Doña Isabel said, still observing her.

"Ok, then. Do you collect coffee?" Marina asked her.

"Of course. This is my farm. It was my husband's as well, but he died two years ago" Doña Isabel answered.

"Sorry for your loss, Doña Isabel. Have a nice day."

Marina started walking back to her vehicle. As Doña Isabel followed Marina with her eyes, she became even more curious than she already was. She wondered what kind of young woman would want to gather coffee beans, after having bought a brand-new car, still holding its cardboard license plate. Just to inquire, she called her back and offered her the job. She told her that the salary was very low, but it came with accommodations, namely a little cottage in the farmhouse courtyard. Marina believed that the circumstance was perfect. Doña Isabel asked her if she wanted to know how much she was going to pay her, but Marina told her that at that moment she was not interested in knowing. She just wanted to go to her lodge and to be informed on the time she would start working.

Doña Isabel told her that she would wake her up very early in the morning, and then, gave her the keys to the tiny guest house. Isabel was very intrigued by Marina's behavior and she visually followed her as she got into her all-terrain vehicle. The moment she turned down the muddy road on the hillside, Isabel lost sight of her. Then, she went into the house and looked out through the high windows of her kitchen, where she could see the little house where Marina would be staying. She noticed she parked right in front of the small wooden cabin in the courtyard and she continued to observe her every move until she entered the cottage.

Once inside, Marina took her clothes and toiletries backpack off her shoulders, and released a flask of whiskey from her right back pocket. The wooden cabin looked like a dollhouse, because it was much smaller than her personal bathroom in Miami. However, she loved it because it had a beautiful little kitchen with vases filled with deep pink geraniums on the windowsill. There was a table and two chairs, a stove, dishwasher, and a small refrigerator. The bathroom was tiny, but it had everything she needed. She went upstairs to the bedroom. Its windows were placed facing each other on the lateral walls of the bedroom, thus blocking the view from the kitchen of the big house. Marina laid down on the bed and began to fall asleep, when she heard someone knock on the door. It was Doña Isabel who decided to invite her to dinner. Initially, Marina did not accept, not wanting to cause her any inconveniences. However, since she insisted, Marina agreed. When they entered the landlady's big house, she observed that the table was already set with plates, cutlery, and right at the center of the table, the covered food pans. Marina inhaled and told her that everything smelled delicious. Isabel smiled, and waved her hand inviting her to sit down. Then she served her a *pastel*, a *yautía* root and green banana dough with pork stuffing, accompanied by white rice and pink beans. Again, Marina commended her for the exquisite dishes she served her. Isabel acknowledged her show of appreciation regarding her culinary talents. Marina was ready to get up from the table and leave, when a handsome young man entered, followed by a tall woman with long brown hair. Doña Isabel was happy to see her son Ernesto, because she did not expect him until the next day. Marina observed the look the mother gave Violeta, her son's girlfriend. She could tell his mother didn't approve of her.

"Ernesto, son, this is Marina. She is our new coffee picker" Doña Isabel told him with a certain voice inflection, letting her son know that she really liked Marina better than Violeta.

"Nice to meet you, Marina. This is Violeta, my fiancée.

"The pleasure is mine" Marina replied.

As she extended her arm to shake hands with Ernesto, he observed on Marina's wrist, a gold watch with precious stones. Doña Isabel saw it as well for the first time, and she wondered how such an obvious detail had escaped her. But she realized that when she met Marina, what caught her attention was her truck, while her wrist watch was covered by her long sleeve. Regardless of these details, Isabel felt a great connection with the young woman. Unlike Isabel, Violeta looked her up and down with disgust for being in the territory of Ernesto's mother. She was not pleased to see that his future mother-in-law sympathized much more with the stranger than with her, whom she had known for a few months. Not paying any attention to either of them, Marina said goodbye to Isabel and retired to her cottage.

That night she slept like never before. She laid down naked after opening the windows. She enjoyed listening to the *coquíes,* who are little singing frogs, native to the island of Puerto Rico. The frogs' loud song triggered Marina's ability to see the spirits of nature walking around the room. Above all, she saw her birth friends arrive from everywhere. They were the dragonflies that returned to give her a Caribbean hug. They looked different to her from those in Miami, but they were the same. Their caress felt like always, generous and lush and protective. She thought that she could stay in Jayuya all of the rest of her life. Then, she was carried away by the affection of the dragonflies and the cool breeze of the mountain night. She had never slept in the mountains before. That caress of the cool hand of the elevation, seemed to her like the most wonderful and spectacular feeling of any other place. She fell asleep as though she had been rocked like a baby. However, as the temperatures dropped further, she got up and closed the windows. She noticed that the dragonflies had already left and that's how she realized that they did not like the cold.

When she woke up at six in the morning, she put on her jeans, boots and a straw hat to protect her hair and skin from the intense Caribbean sun. She then heard Isabel knocking on the door. She came downstairs, ready to start her job. Doña Isabel was glad that she was so eager to help in the coffee harvesting. She invited her to breakfast, since she had not seen Marina go out to buy food in town. She made her a cup of coffee and some toast with cheese. After breakfast, Marina asked Doña Isabel if she could feed her daily and deduct her meals from her salary. She also told her that if she had no money left to collect, there would be no problem, since it was not lack of money what brought her there.

"It was my desire to experience different perspectives in life, that brought me here" Marina told her while taking off her hat to braid her hair.

"I see. You're just passing by. Right?"

Marina was very honest and told Doña Isabel that her intention was to spend no more than two weeks in the mountains, as she hoped to return to her residence in Old San Juan. Doña Isabel smiled, and asked her to just call her Isabel, because calling her by the respectful title of Doña, made her feel too old and serious. Marina then asked her to see a friend in her, who had just come to help her with the coffee harvest. Marina also told her that she wanted to know if she would welcome her with open arms whenever she decided to visit her. Isabel answered that she would always be welcomed no matter how many years passed by. She also asked Marina, if she would also welcome her anytime, regardless of wherever she lived at the time. Marina promised to always welcome her regardless of her circumstances. Then, they embraced each other, creating a bond for life.

After breakfast, they went to work. Marina collected the coffee with determination and care, following every step of the instructions that Isabel had explained to her. She saw that Isabel had other local workers picking coffee at the site, and she became aware that her coffee-selling business, although not very large, was prosperous and profitable. Marina asked Isabel if she would like to sell her coffee in Miami, as she had many contacts in the city. Her new friend informed her that all coffee was consumed locally, but that she would consider her offer as an option for the future, because she knew it was a great idea. However, she would wait to get to know Marina more before venturing to accept her proposal because she needed to know more about her background. They talked at times while they collected the red grains under the radiant light of the sun that blesses and caresses everything that grows. Marina was very satisfied seeing how much coffee she was able to collect. Because it was such a tangible and tactile task, she was very happy to do it. Therefore, she worked until she was exhausted.

Once she finished her long hours of work, she went to a stream quite distant from the well-known landmark *Written*

Stone of the Taíno Indians to have some privacy. There, she took off her shirt, pants, hat, boots and socks; leaving on only her underwear. Then, she jumped into the water and felt the caressing touch of the crystal waters that poured out from the belly of the mountains. She laid down on the stone banks and fell asleep due to the exhaustion she felt from her hours of hard work. Dragonflies came from everywhere to cover her body like flies do over rotten meat. A boy from the area, who was returning from his work, saw her lying there. Observing that she was covered by the swarm, he ran to seek help. Many people found out about the event almost immediately. They called the media, and within an hour, Marina was inadvertently surrounded by a crowd. Even Isabel had come, but she didn't know who the *dead* woman in the stream was, because the crowd did not allow her to get close to her.

After touching her several times and feeling that she was still warm, they concluded that she had just died. Yet, still asleep, Marina turned over from one side to the other. Those still watching, began to scream in terror. Then, she woke up suddenly, scared by the screams. Believing that the deceased was returning from the dead, some fled horrified.

"They turned her into a zombie!" someone in the crowd, yelled.

Feeling besieged by so many people scandalized by seeing her full of dragonflies, Marina began to scare them off, and quickly dress. She regretted not being aware that there were people living nearby. She would have loved to be left alone to continue enjoying her deep sleep and her winged friends. Yet, above all, she felt violated. The intruders had ripped apart the veil of her secret.

Her photo appeared in the newspapers next day under the headline: *The Dragonfly Woman*. The incident depressed her so much that she secretly disappeared from Jayuya, never to return. She felt that she was losing Isabel's friendship forever, because she could not even say goodbye to her, or thank her for her kindness. In short, she never imagined that the first time someone saw her covered in dragonflies, it would be such an embarrassing event in her life. Despite it all, the one thing she feared most was the vulnerability of being recognized by someone in any part of the country.

"Maybe it's better to go back home to Miami" Marina thought, deeply upset and disappointed.

She disguised herself to return to San Juan and hid for a week, as terrified as a cat cornered in an alley by a gang of stray dogs. To go out briefly, she wore wigs and changed her fashion style every day. After her confinement, she opened the doors to allow the salty breezes of the ocean air to enter her apartment. She stepped out into the balcony and ran into Doña Marta, who assessed her altered appearance. After a casual and unexpected greeting from the lady, Marina felt at ease. It was evident that she had let go of the resentment of their previous encounter. Then again, Marina thought that had she been mistaken, perhaps her neighbor Marta was pondering if she was the dragonfly woman seen in Jayuya.

Avoiding to step into a conversation, Marina ventured out to *Parque de las Palomas*. During her walk, she did not hear anyone talking about the news in Jayuya. When she arrived at the Chapel of Christ and turned into the adjoining park, she found her best friend. He saw her wearing dark glasses and a red wig. Although she was disguised, he spread his arms widely as he waved his hands, inviting her to come closer. She walked towards the octogenarian, and they both hugged each other. Don Fernando let her know that no matter how she disguised herself, he would always recognize her.

"Does that mean that you know what happened to me?" Marina asked him.

"First of all, I want you to call me grandfather. We agreed on that. I know that now you need one, and since I also need to have a little granddaughter, that's what you are going to be for me" Don Fernando said emphatically.

Marina asked him to tell her if he knew what had happened. Don Fernando told her that he was probably the only person in the world who knew that she was the *dragonfly woman*. He asked her not to worry so much, because the photos had a poor quality and they did not look like her at all. He asked her not to wear *those ridiculous wigs* to protect herself, because she was not in any danger. Marina took her wig and her sunglasses off, and left them on a park bench for whoever wanted them. She took her grandfather's word regarding the outcome of the event. After walking with him through Old San Juan, she was convinced that he was right. She felt that she could breathe freely and stay in the capital without major mishaps. She took her whiskey flask out of her pocketbook and took a sip. Then she offered some to Don Fernando.

"No thanks. You know what? Please, don't drink that crap. It hurts everything inside of you…even your mind."

Marina put the flask away without arguing, knowing that grandpa was absolutely right. Then, Don Fernando invited Marina to go down to San Juan's neighborhood *La*

Perla (The Pearl), to visit his cousin Cesáreo. Having regained her usual confidence, Marina crossed the colonial belly of San Juan with her grandfather, until they reached the highest area of Norzagaray Street. Then they descended towards the coast by the road that gives access to the neighborhood. She felt comfortable walking through this area located on the outskirts of the colonial walls, since Don Fernando was well-known in La Perla. In no time, they reached Cesáreo's little house, which had been built by him almost on the shore of the ocean.

The salty wind from the Atlantic blew like a giant, invisible fan that flapped the skirts of women in the street and Marina's long hair. Cesáreo was smoking, sitting at his tiny balcony, which was occasionally kissed by the foam of the waves crashing against the reefs of the shore. The smell of his island tobacco dispersed like the outstretched arms of a famous tenor at the end of his best concert. It mingled with the fresh and salty scent of the Atlantic. Cesáreo believed that offering his smoke, was his way to acknowledge the ocean's blue glory. It was an honor for him to be there to thank the majestic ocean for allowing him to express himself right before its imposing presence. In this setting of magical beauty, Don Fernando's tiny and wrinkled relative closed his eyes, hypnotized by the enchantment of the ocean and his Puerto Rican cigar. Don Fernando saw him and made himself heard, thus disturbing the inner reverence of his tiny cousin.

"Always bewitched by tobacco" Don Fernando said smiling at him.

"Never, only the salty breeze of the ocean can do that," Cesáreo said, waking up from his bliss.

"Of course. That is why you are almost one hundred years old."

"Well said. Let's go in for coffee. You know that Xuralia is an excellent barista. This girl…who is she?" Cesáreo asked with curiosity, looking at Marina.

Don Fernando introduced her as his granddaughter and the older man smiled at her. Marina was curious about the man who was less than five feet tall, very thin and shorter than the longest billiard cue. However, he had a wonderful glow. She could tell he was an amazing person. When Cesáreo invited them into his house, Marina was impressed with everything around her. She could barely speak. It seemed inconceivable to her that Don Fernando had not told her anything before about his cousin and his house. She looked at him as though asking him such a question, but he didn't notice her astonishment. Her friend greeted Xuralia, who was sitting on the beautiful couch in the anteroom. Then he introduced her to Marina, who smiled at her, trying to hide a bit how fascinated she was. Xuralia smiled at Marina and winked at her.

"Go downstairs with Cesáreo, while I prepare some delicious coffee for you" she said looking at Fernando and Marina.

Then the three of them descended into the hidden rooms. The upper floor was only a furnished receiving hall, where the handrail of the spiral staircase carved in the original stone, began. It led to the rooms of a very spacious interior house. It was originally an underground reef cavern, with a wide and deep cavity. Everything inside the house smelled of the sea, but the only opening in the reef was the small upper room. This had been camouflaged with a concrete facade to appear to be a small house. However, it was only an impression to the outside world.

Marina was dumbfounded at the hidden natural beauty, decorated in a very contemporary way, in the style of the eighties. She noted that the owners had been very respectful of the original appearance of the rooms, as the ceilings and interior walls displayed their intact reef texture and followed its natural contour. Light entered through several skylights deployed to the outside, simulating natural palm trees. The pipes and the solar panel system, as well as the interior construction, had been created by Cesáreo over several decades.

Xuralia and Cesáreo had been married two days after meeting, twenty years ago. In his eighty years, prior to meeting her, he had never fallen in love. Love surprised him on a summer night, full of greenish lights and lightning. He was driving under a busy bridge in the San Juan metropolitan area, when he suddenly saw a refrigerator box. He found himself parking his car to find out what was making the cartons move from one side to the other. When he looked inside, he saw a marble-skinned Valkyrie that seemed to have come through an astral portal… straight from Valhalla. She was ragged and very dirty, but he knew that she was the woman he had been looking for all his life, although he never imagined she would be blonde, nor three times his size. That night the Valkyrie went to live with Cesáreo.

"Since then, she always carries me and puts me to sleep at bedtime" Cesáreo laughed as he revealed that, which until then, was a secret for his family and friends.

Marina was amused as she listened to Cesáreo's very strange story. She felt that he had entered the dimension of the absurd, since his house and everything related to the couple was unusual, but amazingly wonderful. When Don

Fernando saw that Marina seemed a little confused, he reassured her by letting her know that his entire family was very peculiar.

"You should feel very comfortable with my people. If we saw you covered in dragonflies, none of us would think that there's anything strange about you."

"Grandpa, you are truly wise. You have to meet my sister Silvana. She also gets full of dragonflies" Marina said smiling and feeling very relaxed with Don Fernando and his family.

All of a sudden, Doña Marta was worried about her neighbor since she had not seen her for a while. Therefore, she decided to knock on the door and call her by name. Marina asked her to go to her balcony and speak to her from a distance. She asked her to do so because she considered Marta a very volatile person, and she was a little afraid of her. Doña Marta agreed, aware that Marina's opinion of her, was very true. Marta knew to her dismay, that at times, she could become an unpleasant and abusive person. When she saw Marina this time, Marta gave her a fresh fruit tart that she had confectioned for her, as a way to make peace with her. She even asked Marina to share it with Don Fernando. At that moment, Marta's action reminded her of Felipa Isabel. In the aspect of affection, both were the same, indirect and very repressed.

"…as if being a loving person is a sign of weakness. That action is truly a big turn" Marina thought, while realizing that Marta, just like Felipa Isabel, was a woman who had her feelings suffocated in the depths of her being.

Marina couldn't blame Marta for anything, accepting that her personality could be compared to a volcano. Even in spite of knowing and accepting that fact, Marta's volatility of character caused Marina a great deal of discomfort, and for that reason, she sometimes avoided her. However, in a moment of melancholy when she missed Serena and Silvana, it occurred to her to give Doña Marta her home phone number in Miami.

"You are a very weird and strange girl. You seem to have no sympathy for me, but then right after, you entrust me with your sister's telephone number," Marina remembered Doña Marta telling her while the lady dropped her jaw in disbelief.

"You hit my friend and it was unfair, but that doesn't mean that I do not understand you, or that you do not care. I only ask that in case something bad happens to me, you tell my sister and my mom. Who knows? Despite liking being here, thinking about them makes me want to go back to Miami."

"Oh, Marina! You surely know how to live too fast" Doña Marta commented regarding her constant coming and going.

That same afternoon, Marina started walking aimlessly. She walked for miles, arriving at an unknown place in Santurce. She sat on one of the benches of a wide avenue sidewalk, installed by the city for pedestrians and passengers awaiting a metropolitan bus. There she watched the buses riding in the opposite direction of the lanes assigned to motorists. She wondered how many people would have lost their lives in the first years of buses traveling in the opposite direction, before full public awareness of the change became a norm. She was very grateful to be seated and witness the process. She was learning something that had she not known, could have been fatal for her as well.

"I think I am a very fragile person. Oh my God! Who thinks about those things?" she wondered.

She remained seating there for a long time watching the vehicles come and go. She did not notice that a man in his thirties was watching her, as she remained absorbed in her thoughts. He approached her, but she did not acknowledge his presence. Then, he sat next to her and told her that his name was Marcos.

"I see. Marcos means frames…like the ones on the doors," Marina replied indifferently.

Faced with such unusual comparison, he did not know what to answer. Yet, he remained seated next to her. Ten minutes later, Marina got up and he walked behind her. She went into a cafeteria and he sat at the same table. Marina ignored him and ordered a plate of rice and pink beans with roast chicken, a salad, and a passion fruit juice. Afterwards, she ordered cheese custard and a glass of water. She extended her hand to Marcos, indicating that it was his turn to order. He asked for the same, despite not being hungry. When she finished her meal, she got up, thanked him, and started walking away. Marcos paid the bill and walked right behind her.

"Don't you get tired of following people? We already shared an experience together" she told him as she turned to look at his face.

Marcos mentioned that he was very attracted to her and that if she did not object, they could live together. He told her that he had a colonial-style house in the Miramar area of Santurce, and he had a garden full of many kinds of roses, gardenias, and geraniums. Marina, who was very sensorial, saw the flowers in her mind, and she remembered the scent of the gardenias that she had not smelled for so long. Marcos's proposition contained the magical element of being able to once again be surrounded by a flower that exuded the essence of a goddess. Finding no reason to deny his offer, she replied yes. She would go live with him. Then, Marcos grabbed her by the waist and spun her twice in the air, while they both laughed in happiness. Together they walked hand in hand, on their way to Miramar.

After a long journey on foot, they reached the house. Marina was delighted to see the huge balcony and the garden behind the cement four-foot wall that separated the sidewalk from the house. Opening the small iron gate, she walked down the path surrounded by roses and gardenias on both sides. There, she remained for a long time smelling the flowers and fluttering among the plants. She danced as if listening to the waltz of a magnified symphony orchestra in her mind. Marcos watched her as though he could perceive for the first time, the radiance of the colors of dawn. He felt that he could live with her, and love her for the rest of his life. He watched her dance in her garden, eat rose petals, and put gardenias in her hair.

After an almost spiritual union with Eden, Marina looked at Marcos and asked him to invite her inside his residence. It wasn't as big as her Miami mansion, but it was charming and everything about it was to her heart's delight and liking. For a moment, she realized that at some point she would have to invite her grandfather, Xuralia, Cesáreo, and Doña Marta, to meet Marcos. For some reason, he reminded her of Ernesto, whom she could have married, if it weren't for his girlfriend Violeta and also, her terrible incident with the dragonflies. Thinking of all the people she knew in Puerto Rico she questioned the fact that almost all of them were older than she was. She smiled as she recognized that older adults gave her a pleasant sense of protection, just like a firm, soft pillow filled with feathers does. Then, after gazing inside the house and letting her mind fly on the wings of her absurd thoughts, she turned her attention to Marcos again.

They both entered the bedroom. He hugged her and kissed her tenderly. Then he invited her to take a perfumed bubble bath; an invitation Marina couldn't refuse. Knowing that she would have to get undressed, she asked the strong and loving man, to close the windows of the bathroom, the bedroom, as well as all the doors in the house. He agreed without any hesitation or question. Already facing the tub, she took his shirt off and then, she decided to get undressed. Piece after piece, her garments fell to the ground like boat sails floating down the halyards. Amid the bubbles in the tub, they twisted like octopuses carried over the waves to the foam on the shore.

Then Marcos pulled her out of the tub, entangled in a fluffy white towel. He carried her to his bed, where they made love under the soft rays of light seeping through the glass. The light danced with its faint orange tones on the silken skin of their exposed bodies. Marcos's fingers played the black harp of Marina's thick hair, while the luminous forest of her feminine eyes reflected the look of the man who sheltered in her. He was captive in her crystalline prison; his jailer unaware of his capture. Thus, Eros had witnessed for a week his manifestation through a pair of lovers chosen at random.

After the seventh day, Marina began to feel restricted and decided to leave while Marcos slept. She was slipping off his hands and disappearing as quickly as he had found her. She walked to San Juan, tired, confused, and dehydrated from the cruel lashes of the Caribbean sun.

Silvana and Matthew had been waiting for two days, giving her the opportunity to show up before calling the authorities. As per Doña Marta, Marina's basic pattern of operation was to escape for a few days or sometimes a week, and then return. After observing her behavior on several occasions and fearing for her well-being, she had notified Silvana of his recent disappearance. Marta had understood that when Marina offered her Silvana's information, she was asking for help before her departure. Whether she was right or wrong, after a couple of days missing, her intuition led her to calling her twin sister. As Marina turned right to the corner of her street, Silvana immediately noticed she was upset. Feeling her sister's emotions, Silvana ran downstairs followed by her husband. She opened the two large wooden entry doors of the colonial building. Upon seeing Marina, Silvana hugged her and then, helped her to go upstairs. She could barely speak due to her physical wear and tear.

Doña Marta prepared a jar of very cold tea with lots of lemon for them, and then left, allowing them to discuss their family situation. They sat around the dining room table, where Silvana put the pitcher of tea and the crystal glasses. The tasty local lemon flavor of the tea, revived Marina in an instant.

"You are pregnant, Silvana! What a joy!" she said to her sister, touching her belly.

"I had already told you about it last time we spoke on the phone."

"But I hadn't seen you. I can only tell by looking at your face. Your belly has barely grown."

"Don't you think it's time to go back home? Silvana asked her sister.

"Yes, I want to go now …but what do I do with this apartment and my truck?"

"Mathew will take care of that. Get your things ready. We'll be leaving today" Silvana answered, pouring some more tea from the jug.

Marina looked around but she really didn't have much to take with her. Therefore, she stuffed her backpack with the same things she had arrived. She then said goodbye to Doña Marta and asked her to tell Don Fernando that she would soon return to see him. Both neighboring women hugged and kissed each other on the cheek.

"I will never forget you, Doña Marta. You know, despite all our differences, I learned to love you very much" Marina said teary eyed.

"I love you too, my daughter."

Within a few hours, Mathew and the sisters were flying back to Miami. Silvana asked her sister why she had not gone to Ponce to visit Manuel and Elena. Marina replied that she was afraid of reliving the terrible experience of losing her parents.

"It still is an open wound in my heart" Marina answered regretfully. She wished the couple that had such a great impact in her upbringing had not found out about her short sojourn on the island. Silvana immediately eliminated her concern by telling her that neither she, nor Serena, had notified them.

Upon arriving in Miami, Marina found Serena waiting for her, standing right in front of the wide doors of the mansion.

"It is so good to see you again, my beautiful girl!" Serena said with tears on her eyes, hugging her.

Marina kissed her on her right cheek while Serena held her tightly. Marina asked her not to cry and told her that she prayed for her every day, because she always felt her presence in her soul regardless of place and time. Yet, for Serena and Marina, their brief separation felt as though they hadn't seen each other in many, many years, even though Marina had only been in Puerto Rico for less than two months. No one asked her anything, nor did they question the reason for her departure. It was enough for them to remember that she always wanted to know the country of her parents. Regardless of other reasons no one needed to know, Marina was happy to be back. She simply put her backpack on an armchair, went to her room and after taking an amazing bath, she slept for two days as though she had returned from India.

On the third day she awoke very refreshed, just at dinner time. Lucia, the new cook Silvana had hired, had prepared all of Marina's favorite dishes. She thanked the new cook and then, sat down at the table to enjoy the company of her family and the dishes Lucia had prepared for her. She pulled out her flask from one of her pockets, to take a sip of whiskey. With a simple facial sign, Silvana alerted her not to do it again. Marina abstained while at the table. Then, she noticed Lawrence.

"And…who are you?" she asked, unaware that they had met in the past.

"You do not remember me?"

Silvana intervened and reminded her sister that he had asked her out on the night of her wedding. Marina did not remember the incident. However, she apologized to him. She had worked too hard on the preparations and her exhaustion was surely the reason for her forgetfulness.

Lawrence smiled at her, understanding that the timing of his invitation had not been practical at all. After dinner, they both sat down to talk, but not before Marina asked Silvana if she knew anything about Luis Segarra.

"I didn't hear from him again. Thank God for that!" Silvana responded, and Marina smiled at her feeling very pleased with her answer.

After a few days of his visit to the mansion, Lawrence asked Marina out again, and she agreed. Silvana was pleased and also realized that her sister was feeling stronger. Therefore, after a week and a half, she decided to tell Marina about Serena's health. However, she had already noticed that her nanny looked much more deteriorated than before she had left. She had also realized that her condition made her look much older than forty-five. However, Silvana explained to her sister that her condition had currently deteriorated into a metastasized cancer. They had discovered the magnitude of her present situation just over a month ago, for which she had started to receive a very aggressive treatment with limited encouraging results.

"I think I was in denial. I wanted to fool myself not to lose her" Marina told her sister, realizing that she had always suspected Serena's ailment.

"I know, Marina. The same happened to me. You know? I've missed you so much! I couldn't do this by myself. I needed you here" Silvana said hugging her.

"I understand. I wouldn't have either" her twin said while crying over her right shoulder.

"Mommy will be leaving us soon!"

Then they continued crying together for a long time, emptying the dam of their painful emotional waters. That same afternoon, Serena lost consciousness. The twins called the doctors, preferring that she died in the comfort of her home. Doctors gave her very strong drugs so that she did not feel any pain. One of the doctors and her nurse stayed by her side, monitoring her process. The twins also spent the whole night next to her. It was ten o'clock in the morning of the next day, when Marina saw Serena's etheric double leaving her body behind. Serena smiled at her with her usual sweetness, saying goodbye. Marina squeezed her sister's left hand, while she continued to look at Serena.

"She's gone, Silvana. Mommy kissed us goodbye."
Silvana walked over to the bed and saw there was no heart beat recorded on the monitor. She closed Serena's eyes with her right hand. The sisters looked at each other and left the room. They didn't want to cry and make her passing a painful time for the departed. They felt that showing

acceptance would make it easier for Serena to move one. That same afternoon, after the doctor certified her death, Marina went out to process the government issued death certificate. Hours later, her remains were taken to the funeral home in preparation for her cremation, as Serena had requested.

The great emptiness that the selfless mother left in the twins' lives was inconceivable to them. Without her, Marina did not want to stay in the mansion, despite worrying about Silvana's emotional state, for she was entering her second trimester of pregnancy. At the same time, Marina felt overwhelmed staying at the mansion with a brother-in-law she hardly knew and with whom she did not share any common interests. In order not to spend too much time at her childhood home, Marina decided to start dating Lawrence more often, three weeks after Serena's funeral. She found him very likable, despite not being attracted to him at all. After dating him for a short while, she remembered that she had entered and disappeared from Marcos' life, like a tropical hurricane. She had no idea why she had done it, because he was the man who had inspired her the most...after Ernesto.

"Perhaps I should call Doña Isabel to find out if he got

married. No, I better forget about all that crazy mess. I cannot, nor do I ever want to show up in Jayuya in my entire life" she thought in the solitude of her bedroom.

Two months after Serena's death, Marina decided to stop the vehicle she had bought in Puerto Rico, at the edge of a bridge in Miami. It was almost four in the morning and she was so drunk that she was essentially out of her senses. Feeling the fiery summer heat, she stripped off her clothes and stood on the edge of the bridge, leaping into the void. She fell into the whooshing water and was carried away without resisting. However, when she emerged, she felt her body fly towards the water's edge.

"Why have they saved me, if I don't mind dying?" she asked the question aloud, as she saw a flight of dragonflies. She listened to their soft sounds attentively. Although unable to discern or explain how, she was able to understand their message.

"We were women who also felt lost. While we wait to reincarnate as humans once again, we agreed to prevent others from doing the same" the dragonflies told Marina. Marina thought she was totally crazy. Upon arriving home, she told Silvana her experience and asked her to confine her to a sanatorium.

* * *

The nurse on duty entered to administer the young woman's medications to begin a new treatment. The doses would be watched closely to determine their effectiveness, as she had been diagnosed as having schizophrenia with suicidal tendencies, and alcoholism. Within three months of her arrival, it was confirmed that the woman was pregnant and it was decided that the patient would require further medical observation. Although the pregnancy took her by surprise, as the days passed, she believed that it was a story made up by the psychiatrists, obstetricians, and all the medical personnel treating her.

Her family felt powerless, given the exacerbation created by her prenatal condition, and the fact that doctors did not offer them concrete or definitive answers. Pregnancy only affected the dosage of the medicine, but also created additional needs for the patient. It had also occurred at a delicate and inopportune moment when the patient was not in control of her mental status. The treatment did not appear to slow the progression of her mental decline and the presence of the new hormones only exacerbated the condition. She barely recognized her loved ones. She also went in and out of different realities as though crossing the divide of human dimensions. It was obvious that she would remain in the Miami sanitarium for a long time.

She saw a woman almost every day who would visit her seeking conversation. She was a volunteer with whom she felt she had a connection, possibly because she brought her international magazines that she loved to read. She learned about the royal family of Spain, and world entertainment; although she would later forget what she had read, or simply misconstrued the facts. She tore photographs to paste them onto cardboard pieces. She would also draw faces, and read paragraphs from classic novels and plays from Spanish literature; their main message and meaning never retained. In addition, she forgot every day who was the generous woman who brought her the reading material. However, whenever she saw her, she realized that she was someone special in her life, because she always came with a gift for her. She also provided her with food that she liked and was allowed to consume. Also, she occasionally brought some clothes that the nurses on duty allowed her to wear, because they met the requirements of use.

Every day, the woman who was in her forties, managed to get closer to her. She would ask her personal questions, but the patient replied with short, incoherent answers. However, she always requested the visiting lady to find out information about Luis Segarra.

"Do you remember him?" the volunteer asked her.

"I don't know, but I recall his name all the time. I think I need to talk to him. How about you…do you know him?"

"He comes every day to see you" the lady replied.

"That's impossible. He is a famous actor and they talk about him a lot in magazines. Please, check that the window is properly closed" she said nervously to the volunteer, while scratching her head.

"Don't worry. The windows can only be pushed one inch in and out."

"Well, don't even open them."

She repeated the conversations often. Forgetting that she had asked the same questions over and over again, she always received the memorized answers by the doctors and the care staff. Afterward, she would fall asleep like a little baby girl in the womb, in a fetal position and with her right thumb in her mouth. This behavior was the constant throughout the months her belly grew. Believing that she was just gaining weight, she rejected food. The nurse on duty had to persuade her that she was pregnant and that if she did not eat nutritious food, she would have health problems. Yet, she agreed to eat only if the nurse sang a song that was in style. Since this was the only thing that convinced her to eat, Beatriz, a nurse who was a very good singer, usually performed the task. If she was not available, the volunteer who came to see her every day, managed to make her eat. Given the fact that both ladies had an evident affinity, the patient ended up accepting her out of tune songs.

Her general treatment had become normalized after her first trimester of gestation. Besides the singing duty, the only complication was her need to cry about almost anything. In addition, she kept asking about Luis Segarra. Doctors and nurses alike were counting the months, the days, and even the hours, for her to give birth. Then, they could be a little more aggressive with their medications, to accomplish a more stabilizing mental status. It was necessary for her to improve psychologically, so that she could learn to care for her two babies, while still in the psychiatric unit. Treatment at home seemed to be an impossible alternative for a while because she had a history of disappearing for days after getting drunk on whiskey. Despite her drinking problem before entering the psychiatric hospital, her taste for alcohol seemed to be manageable. She often begged the nurses for a drink to calm her nerves, but they only gave her juice, and she learned to give up her request without altering her mood.

Its institutional dynamics were always the same. One day was basically a repetition of the previous day, as if her life were a movie shown at the same theater, year after year. However, very rarely observed variants emerged.

Thus began the next day. Before the arrival of the volunteer woman in the morning, she was visited by a very handsome gentleman. He kissed her head and hugged her. She was lost in his chest and while he held her, she closed her eyes and calmed down.

"I'm so happy that you came to see me! The alternate worlds do not allow me to live in peace" she said.

"That doesn't exist, darling. It's only real in your mind."

"No, you must believe me. If not, I would have my twin daughters with me."

"You were very young and we had many problems. It took me so long to know where you went."

"It was something so strange, Luis."

While she relished those moments with her husband, she did not notice that a new nurse, who had just entered her room, had pushed the window open, to ventilate the room. Then, she left without making a sound, just like a little mouse hiding in the corners of an abandoned attic. Luis, who had seen the nurse enter, asked his wife very affectionately, to close her eyes in order to give her a surprise he had brought her. She did as he requested and he got up very slowly. He pushed the window in very gently, so she wouldn't know it had been opened. Then, he took a flower from a vase on the table and walked back to her.

"Soledad, my love, I brought you this fresh rose so that when I go to work, you can remember I came to see you.

"I'm so happy you're here, Luis!"

"Darling, as early as always, your Luis came to see you. I'll be back tomorrow to check how you and the twins are doing."

Luis Segarra went to work like did every day, but he did not notice that a dragonfly, larger than usual, had slipped through the gap in the bedroom window. When he left, the dragonfly settled on Soledad's chest. Without her feeling its presence, Soledad fell asleep, never to wake up again. Meanwhile, in the same corridor of Soledad's room, a new patient was crying out loud. She had just been admitted and was taken to the room next to Soledad's, after tests and initial treatment.

"I'll be fine soon, Silvana. I swear! I love you so much!" Drowning in her tears, Marina scratched her head as she said goodbye to her sister.

"I love you as well. I'll come to see you as often as I can. Please take good care of yourself" her sister Silvana would tell her, trying to understand how she had deteriorated so much mentally; without truly noticing the depths of its severity.